St. Thomas Aquinas

On Prayer and the Contemplative Life

St. Thomas Aquinas

On Prayer and the Contemplative Life

On Prayer

and the

Contemplative Life

by St. Thomas Aquinas

CONTENTS

QUESTION LXXXI

OF THE VIRTUE OF RELIGION

I

Does the Virtue of Religion direct a Man to God Alone?

Cicero says: "Religion offers internal and external reverence to that Superior Nature which we term the Divine."

S. Isidore says: "A religious man is, as Cicero remarks, so called from *religion*, for he is occupied with and, as it were, reads through again and again (*relegit*) the things that concern Divine worship." Thus religion seems to be so called from reading again (*religendo*) things concerning Divine worship; for such things are to be repeatedly revolved in the mind, according to those words of Proverbs iii. 6: *In all thy ways think on Him.* At the same time *religion* might be said to be so called because "we ought to choose again (*re-eligere*) those things which through our negligence we have lost," as S. Augustine has noted. Or perhaps it is better derived from "binding again" (*religando*); thus S. Augustine says: "Let religion bind us once more to the One Almighty God."

But whether religion be so called from frequent *reading*, or from *fresh election* of Him Whom we have negligently lost, or from *rebinding*, it properly implies a certain relation to God. For it is He to Whom we ought to be especially *bound* as our indefectible principle; to Him must we assiduously direct our *choice* as our ultimate end; He it is Whom we negligently lose by sin and Whom we must regain by believing in Him and by professing our faith in Him.

But some deny that religion directs a man to God alone, thus:

1. S. James says: *Religion clean and undefiled before God and the Father is this: to visit the fatherless and widows in their tribulation; and to keep oneself unspotted from this world.* But *to visit the fatherless and widows* indicates relation to our neighbour, and *to keep oneself unspotted from this world* refers to ourselves. Hence religion is not confined to our relationship with God.

But religion has two sorts of acts. Some belong to it properly and immediately, those acts, namely, which it elicits and by which man is directed to God alone, as, for instance, to offer Him sacrifice, to adore Him, etc.

But there are other acts which religion produces through the medium of the virtues which it controls, directing them, that is, towards reverence to God; for that virtue which is concerned with the end directs those virtues which have to do with the means to the end. And in this sense *to visit the fatherless and widows in their tribulation* is said to be an act of religion because commanded by it, though actually elicited by the virtue of mercy. Similarly *to keep*

I

oneself unspotted from this world is an act commanded by religion, though elicited by temperance or some other virtue.

2. S. Augustine says: "Since according to the genius of the Latin speech—and that not merely of the unlearned, but even of the most learned—religion is said to be shown towards our human relatives and connexions and intimates, this word 'religion' cannot be used without some ambiguity when applied to the worship of God; hence we cannot say with absolute confidence that religion is nought else but the worship of God." Religion, then, is not limited to our relation to God, but embraces, our neighbour as well.

But it is only by an extension of the name "religion" that it is made to embrace our relations towards our human kin, it is not according to the proper signification of the word. Hence S. Augustine prefaced the words quoted from him above with the remark: "Religion, strictly speaking, seems to mean, not any kind of worship, but only that of God."

3. Further, *latria* seems to come under religion. But S. Augustine says: "*Latria* is interpreted as service." But we ought to serve not God only, but our neighbour as well: *By charity of the spirit serve one another.* Religion, then, implies relation to our neighbour.

But since a slave implies a master, it follows that where there exists a peculiar and special title of dominion there also will be found a peculiar and special ratio of servitude. It is clear, however, that dominion belongs to God in a peculiar and special fashion, since He it is Who has made all things and Who holds the chief rule over all things. Consequently a special kind of service is due to Him. And this service is by the Greeks designated *latria*, which is, in consequence, properly comprised under "religion."

4. Again, reverence comes under religion. But man has to reverence, not only God, but his neighbour as well; as Cato says: "Reverence parents." Hence religion establishes a relation between ourselves and our neighbour as well as between ourselves and God.

But we are said to reverence those men whom we honour or remember, or to whose presence we resort. So, too, even things which are subject to us are said to be "cultivated" by us (*coli*); thus husbandmen (*agricolæ*) are so called because they "cultivate" the fields; the inhabitants of a place, too (*incolæ*), are so called because they "cultivate" the spots where they dwell. But since special honour is due to God as the First Principle of all, a special kind of "cultus" or "reverence" is His due, and this the Greeks call *eusebia* or *theosebia*, as S. Augustine says.

5. Lastly, all who are in a state of salvation are subject to God. But not all who are in a state of salvation are called "religious," but those only who bind themselves by certain vows and observances and who undertake to obey certain men. Hence religion does not seem to mean the relationship of subjection of man to God.

But although, generally speaking, all those who worship God can be termed "religious," yet those are specially so called who dedicate their whole lives to the Divine worship and cut themselves off from worldly occupations.

Thus those are not termed "contemplatives" who merely contemplate, but they who devote their lives to contemplation. And such men do not subject themselves to men for man's sake, but for God's, as the Apostle says: *You received me as an Angel of God, even as Christ Jesus.*

S. Augustine: We are to abide in Christ! How then shall That not be now our possession Where we are then to abide and Whence we are to draw Life? Let Holy Scripture speak for us lest we should seem in mere conjecture to be saying things contrary to the teaching of the Word of God. Hear the words of one who knew: *If God be for us who is against us? The Lord*, he says, *is the portion of my inheritance.* He saith not: Lord, what wilt Thou give me for mine inheritance? All that Thou canst give me is worthless! Be Thou mine inheritance! Thee do I love! Thee do I wholly love! With all my heart, with all my soul, with all my mind do I love Thee! What, then, shall be my lot? What wilt Thou give me save Thyself? This is to love God freely. This is to hope for God from God. This is to hasten to be filled with God, to be sated with Him. For He is sufficient for thee; apart from Him nought can suffice thee! (*Sermon*, cccxxxiv. 3).

S. Augustine: I cried to the Lord with my voice. Many cry to the Lord that they may win riches, that they may avoid losses; they cry that their family may be established, they ask for temporal happiness, for worldly dignities; and, lastly, they cry for bodily health, which is the patrimony of the poor. For these and suchlike things many cry to the Lord; hardly one cries for the Lord Himself! How easy it is for a man to desire all manner of things from the Lord and yet not desire the Lord Himself! As though the gift could be sweeter than the Giver! (*on Ps.* lxxvi.).

S. Augustine: Picture God as saying to you—He Who re-created you and adopted you: "My son, why is it that day by day you rise and pray, and genuflect, and even strike the ground with your forehead, nay, sometimes even shed tears, while you say to Me: 'My Father, my God! give me wealth!' If I were to give it to you, you would think yourself of some importance, you would fancy you had gained something very great. Yet because you asked for it you have it. But take care to make good use of it. Before you had it you were humble; now that you have begun to be rich you despise the poor! What kind of a good is that which only makes you worse? For worse you are, since you were bad already. And that it would make you worse you knew not, hence you asked it of Me. I gave it to you and I proved you; you have found—and you are found out! You were hidden when you had nothing. Correct thyself! Vomit up this cupidity! Take a draught of charity!... Ask of Me better things than these, greater things than these. Ask of Me spiritual things. Ask of Me Myself!" (*Sermon*, cccxi. 14-15).

II

Is Religion a Virtue?

A virtue is that which both renders its possessor, as also his work, good. Hence we must say that every good act comes under virtue. And it is clear that to render to another what is his due has the character of a good act; for by the fact that a man renders to another his due there is established a certain fitting proportion and order between them. But order comes under the ratio of good, just as do measure and species, as S. Augustine establishes. Since, then, it belongs to religion to render to some one, namely, God, the honour which is His due, it is clear that religion is a virtue.

Some, however, deny this, thus:

1. It belongs to religion to show reverence to God. But reverence is an act of fear, and fear is a gift. Religion, then, is a gift, not a virtue.

To reverence God is indeed an act of the gift of fear. But to religion it belongs to do certain things by reason of our reverence for God. Hence it does not follow that religion is the same thing as the gift of fear, but it is related to it as to a higher principle. For the gifts are superior to the moral virtues.

2. All virtue consists in the free-will, and hence virtue is called an elective or voluntary habit. But *latria* belongs to religion, and *latria* implies a certain servitude. Hence religion is not a virtue.

But even a servant can freely give to his master the service that is his due and thus "make a virtue of necessity" by voluntarily paying his debt. And similarly the payment of due service to God can be an act of virtue according as a man does it voluntarily.

3. Lastly, as is said in Aristotle's *Ethics,* the aptitude for the virtues is implanted in us by nature; hence those things which come under the virtues arise from the dictates of natural reason; but it belongs to religion to offer external reverence to the Divine Nature. Ceremonial, however, or external reverence, is not due to the dictates of natural reason. Hence religion is not a virtue. But it is due to the dictates of natural reason that a man does certain things in order to show reverence to God. That he should do precisely this or that, however, does not come from the dictates of natural reason, but from Divine or human positive law.

III

Is Religion One Virtue?

S. Paul says to the Ephesians: *One God, one faith.* But true religion maintains faith in one God. Consequently religion is one virtue.

Habits are distinguished according to the divers objects with which they are concerned. But it belongs to religion to show reverence for the One God for one particular reason, inasmuch, namely, as He is the First Principle, the Creator and Governor of all things; hence we read in Malachi: *If I am a Father, where is my honour?* for it is the father that produces and governs. Hence it is clear that religion is but one virtue.

But some maintain that religion is not one virtue, thus:

1. By religion we are ordained to God. But in God there are Three Persons, and, moreover, divers attributes which are at least distinguishable from one another by reason. But the diverse character of the objects on which they fall suffices to differentiate the virtues. Hence religion is not one virtue.

But the Three Divine Persons are but One Principle as concerns the creation and the government of things. And consequently They are to be served by one religion. And the divers attributes all concur in the First Principle, for God produces all and governs all by His Wisdom, His Will, and the power of His Goodness. Hence religion is but one virtue.

2. One virtue can have but one act; for habits are differentiated according to their acts. But religion has many acts, *e.g.*, to worship, to serve, to make vows, to pray, to make sacrifices, and many other similar things. Consequently religion is not one virtue.

But by one and the same act does man serve God and worship Him; for worship is referred to God's excellence, to which is due reverence: service regards man's subjection, for by reason of his condition he is bound to show reverence to God. And under these two heads are comprised all the acts which are attributed to religion; for by them all man makes protestation of the Divine excellence and of his subjection of himself to God, either by offering Him something, or, again, by taking upon himself something Divine.

3. Further, adoration belongs to religion. But adoration is paid to images for one reason and to God for another. But since diversity of "reason" serves to differentiate the virtues, it seems that religion is not one virtue. But religious worship is not paid to images considered in themselves as entities, but precisely as images bringing God Incarnate to our mind. Further, regarding an image precisely as an image of some one, we do not stop at it; it carries us on to that which it represents. Hence the fact that religious veneration is paid to images of Christ in no sense means that there are various kinds of *latria*, nor different virtues of religion.

IV

Is Religion a Special Virtue Distinct From Others?

Religion is regarded as a part of Justice, and is distinct from the other parts of Justice.

Since virtue is ordained to what is good, where there exists some special ratio of good there must be some special corresponding virtue. But the particular good towards which religion is ordained is the showing due honour to God. Honour, however, is due by reason of some excellency. And to God belongs pre-eminent excellence, since He in every possible way infinitely transcends all things. Hence special honour is due to Him; just as we note that in human concerns varying honours are due to the varying excellencies of persons; one is the honour of a father, another that of a king, and so on. Hence it is manifest that religion is a special virtue.

Some, however, maintain that religion is not a special virtue distinct from others, thus:

1. S. Augustine says: "True sacrifice is every work undertaken in order that we may be joined to God in holy fellowship." But sacrifice comes under religion. Every work of virtue therefore comes under religion. And consequently it is not a special virtue.

But every work of virtue is said to be a sacrifice in so far as it is directed to showing God reverence. It does not thence follow that religion is a general virtue, but that it commands all the other virtues.

2. The Apostle says to the Corinthians: *Do all to the glory of God.* But it belongs to religion to do some things for the glory of God. Hence religion is not a special virtue.

But all kinds of acts, in so far as they are done for the glory of God, come under religion; not, however, as though it elicited them, but inasmuch as it controls them. Those acts, however, come under religion as eliciting them which, by their own specific character, pertain to the service of God.

3. Lastly, the charity whereby we love God is not distinct from the charity by which we love our neighbour. But in the *Ethics* it is said: "To be honoured is akin to being loved." Hence religion by which God is honoured is not a specifically distinct virtue from those observances, whether *dulia* or piety, whereby we honour our neighbour. Hence it is not a special virtue.

But the object of love is a *good* thing; whereas the object of honour or reverence is what is *excellent.* But it is God's Goodness that is communicated to His creatures, not the excellence of His Goodness. Hence while the charity wherewith we love God is not a distinct virtue from the charity wherewith we love our neighbour, yet the religion whereby we honour God is distinct from the virtues whereby we honour our neighbour.

V

Is Religion One of the Theological Virtues?

Religion is considered a part of Justice, and this is a moral virtue.

Religion is the virtue whereby we offer to God His due honour. Two things have therefore to be considered in religion. First we have to consider what religion offers God, namely, worship: this may be regarded as the material and the object with which religion is concerned.

6

Secondly, we have to consider Him to Whom it is offered, namely, God Himself. Now, when worship is offered to God it is not as though our worshipful acts touched God, though this is the case when we believe God, for by believing in God we touch Him (and we have therefore said elsewhere that God is the object of our faith not simply inasmuch as we believe in God, but inasmuch as we believe God). Due worship, however, is offered to God in that certain acts whereby we worship Him are performed as homage to Him, the offering sacrifice, for instance, and so forth. From all which it is evident that God does not stand to the virtue of religion as its object or as the material with which it is concerned, but as its goal. And consequently religion is not a theological virtue, for the object of these latter is the ultimate end; but religion is a moral virtue, and the moral virtues are concerned with the means to the end.

But some regard religion as a theological virtue, thus:

1. S. Augustine says: "God is worshipped by faith, hope, and charity," and these are theological virtues. But to offer worship to God comes under religion. Therefore religion is a theological virtue.

But it is always the case that a faculty or a virtue whose object is a certain end, controls—by commanding—those faculties or virtues which have to do with those things which are means to that end. But the theological virtues—*i.e.*, faith, hope, and charity—are directly concerned with God as their proper object. And hence they are the cause—by commanding it—of the act of the virtue of religion which does certain things having relation to God. It is in this sense that S. Augustine says that "God is worshipped by faith, hope, and charity."

2. Those are called theological virtues which have God for their object. But religion has God for its object, for it directs us to God alone. Therefore it is a theological virtue.

But religion directs man to God, not indeed as towards its object, but as towards its goal.

3. Lastly, every virtue is either theological or intellectual or moral. But religion is not an intellectual virtue, for its perfection does not consist in the consideration of the truth. Neither is it a moral virtue, for the property of the moral virtues is to steer a middle course betwixt what is superfluous and what is below the requisite; whereas no one can worship God to excess, according to the words of Ecclesiasticus: *For He is above all praise.* Religion, then, can only be a theological virtue.

But religion is neither an intellectual nor a theological virtue, but a moral virtue, for it is part of justice. And the *via media* in religion lies, not between the passions, but in a certain harmony which it establishes in the acts which are directed towards God. I say "a certain," not an absolute harmony, for we can never show to God all the worship that is His due; I mean, then, the harmony arising from the consideration of our human powers and of the Divine acceptance of what we offer. Moreover, there can be excess in those things which have to do with the Divine worship; not indeed as regards quantity, but in certain other circumstances, as, for example, when Divine worship is offered to whom it should not, or at times when it should not, or in other unfitting circumstances.

VI

Is Religion to be preferred to the Other Moral Virtues?

In Exodus the commandments which concern religion are put first, as though they were of primary importance. But the order of the commandments is proportioned to the order of the virtues; for the commandments of the Law fall upon the acts of the virtues. Hence religion is chief among the moral virtues.

The means to an end derive their goodness from their relation to that end; hence the more nigh they are to the end the better they are. But the moral virtues are concerned with those things which are ordained to God as their goal. And religion approaches more nearly to God than do the other moral virtues, inasmuch as it is occupied with those things which are directly and immediately ordained to the Divine honour. Hence religion is the chief of the moral virtues.

Some, however, deny that religion is pre-eminent among the moral virtues, thus:

1. The perfection of a moral virtue lies in this, that it keeps the due medium. But religion fails to attain the medium of justice, for it does not render to God anything absolutely equal to Him. Hence religion is not better than the other moral virtues.

But the praiseworthiness of a virtue lies in the will, not in the power. Hence to fall short of equality—which is the midpath of justice—for lack of power, does not make virtue less praiseworthy, provided the deficiency is not due to the will.

2. Again, in our service of men a thing seems to be praiseworthy in proportion to the need of him whom we assist; hence it is said in Isaias: *Deal thy bread to the hungry.* But God needs nothing that we can offer Him, according to the Psalmist: *I have said: Thou art my God, for Thou hast no need of my goods.* Hence religion seems to be less praiseworthy than the other virtues, for by them man is succoured.

But in the service we render to another for his profit, that is the more praiseworthy which is rendered to the most needy, because it is of greater profit to him. But no service is rendered to God for His profit—for His glory, indeed, but for our profit.

3. Lastly, the greater the necessity for doing a thing the less worthy it is of praise, according to the words: *For if I preach the Gospel, it is no glory to me, for a necessity lieth upon me.* But the greater the debt the greater the necessity. Since, then, the service which man offers to God is the greatest of debts, it would appear that religion is the least praiseworthy of all human virtues.

8

Where necessity comes in the glory of supererogation is non-existent; but the merit of the virtue is not thereby excluded, provided the will be present. Consequently the argument does not follow.

VII

Has Religion, That is *Latria*, any External Acts?

In Ps. lxxxiii. 3 it is said: *My heart and my flesh have rejoiced in the living God.* Now interior acts belong to the heart, and in the same way exterior acts are referred to the members of the body. It appears, then, that God is to be worshipped by exterior as well as by interior acts.

We do not show reverence and honour to God for His own sake—for He in Himself is filled with glory to which nought can be added by any created thing—but for our own sakes. For by the fact that we reverence and honour God our minds are subjected to Him, and in that their perfection lies; for all things are perfected according as they are subjected to that which is superior to them—the body, for instance, when vivified by the soul, the air when illumined by the sun. Now the human mind needs—if it would be united to God—the guidance of the things of sense; for, as the Apostle says to the Romans: *The invisible things of Him are clearly seen, being understood by the things that are made.* Hence in the Divine worship it is necessary to make use of certain corporal acts, so that by their means, as by certain signs, man's mind may be stirred up to those spiritual acts whereby it is knit to God. Consequently religion has certain interior acts which are its chief ones and which essentially belong to it; but it has also external acts which are secondary and which are subordinated to the interior acts.

Some deny, however, that exterior acts belong to religion or *latria*, thus:

1. In S. John iv. 24 we read: *For God is a Spirit, and they that adore Him must adore Him in spirit and in truth.* External acts belong, however, rather to the body than to the spirit. Consequently religion, which comprises adoration, has no exterior acts, but only interior.

But here the Lord speaks only of that which is chiefest and which is essentially intended in Divine worship.

2. The end of religion is to show reverence and honour to God. But it is not reverent to offer to a superexcellent person what properly belongs to inferiors. Since, then, what a man offers by bodily acts seems more in accordance with men's needs and with that respect which we owe to inferior created beings, it does not appear that it can fittingly be made use of in order to show reverence to God.

But such external acts are not offered to God as though He needed them, as He says in the Psalm: *Shall I eat the flesh of bullocks? Or shall I drink the blood of goats?* But such acts are offered to God as signs of those interior and spiritual works which God accepts for their own sakes. Hence S. Augustine says: "The visible sacrifice is the sacrament—that is, the visible sign—of the invisible sacrifice."

3. Lastly, S. Augustine praises Seneca for his condemnation of those men who offered to their idols what they were wont to offer to men: on the ground, namely, that what belongs to mortal men is not fittingly offered to the immortals. Still less, then, can such things be fittingly offered to the True God Who is *above all gods*. Therefore to worship God by means of bodily acts seems to be reprehensible. And consequently religion does not include bodily acts.

But idolaters are so called because they offer to their idols things belonging to men, and this not as outward signs which may excite in them spiritual affections, but as being acceptable by those idols for their own sake. And especially because they offered them empty and vile things.

S. Augustine: When men pray, they, as becomes suppliants, make use of their bodily members, for they bend the knee, they stretch forth their hands, they even prostrate on the ground and perform other visible acts. Yet all the while their invisible will and their heart's intention are known to God. He needs not these signs for the human soul to be laid bare before Him. But man by so doing stirs himself up to pray and groan with greater humility and fervour. I know not how it is that whereas such bodily movements can only be produced by reason of some preceding act on the part of the soul, yet when they are thus visibly performed the interior invisible movement which gave them birth is thereby itself increased, and the heart's affections—which must have preceded, else such acts would not have been performed—are thereby themselves increased.

Yet none the less, if a man be in some sort hindered so that he is not at liberty to make use of such external acts, the interior man does not therefore cease to pray; in the secret chamber of his heart, where lies compunction, he lies prostrate before the eyes of God (*Of Care for the Dead*, v.).

VIII

Is Religion the Same as Sanctity?

In S. Luke's Gospel we read: *Let us serve Him in holiness and justice.* But to serve God comes under religion. Hence religion is the same as sanctity.

The word "sanctity" seems to imply two things. First, it seems to imply *cleanness*, and this is in accordance with the Greek word for it, for in Greek it is *hagios*, as though meaning "without earth." Secondly, it implies *stability*, and thus among the ancients those things were termed *sancta* which were so hedged about with laws that they were safe from violation; similarly a thing is said to be *sancitum* because established by law. And even according to the Latins the word *sanctus* may mean "cleanness," as derived from *sanguine tinctus*, for of old those who were to be purified were sprinkled with the blood of a victim, as says S. Isidore in his *Etymologies.*

And both meanings allow us to attribute sanctity to things which are used in the Divine worship; so that not men only, but also temples and vessels and other similar things are said to be sanctified by reason of their use in Divine worship. *Cleanness* indeed is necessary if a man's mind is to be applied to God. For the mind of man is stained by being immersed in inferior things, as indeed all things are cheapened by admixture with things inferior to them—silver, for instance, when mixed with lead. And for our minds to be knit to the Supreme Being they must needs be withdrawn from inferior things. Without cleanness, then, the mind cannot be applied to God. Hence in the Epistle to the Hebrews it is said: *Follow peace with all men, and holiness, without which no man shall see God.*

Stability is also required if the mind is to be applied to God. For the mind is applied to Him as to the Ultimate End and First Principle, and consequently must be immovable. Hence the Apostle says: *For I am sure that neither death nor life shall separate me from the love of God.*

Sanctity, then, is said to be that whereby man's mind and its acts are applied to God. Hence sanctity does not differ from religion essentially, but in idea only. For by religion we mean that a man offers God due service in those things which specially pertain to the Divine worship—sacrifices, for example, and oblations, etc.; but by sanctity we mean that a man not only offers these things, but also refers to God the works of the other virtues, and also that a man disposes himself by good works for the Divine worship.

Some, however, deny the identity of religion and sanctity, thus:

1. Religion is a certain special virtue. But sanctity is called a general virtue, for according to Andronicus, sanctity is that which "makes men faithful observers of what is justly due to God." Hence sanctity is not the same as religion.

But sanctity is in its essence a special virtue, and as such is, in a sort, the same as religion. It has, however, a certain general aspect in that, by its commands, it directs all the acts of the virtues to the Divine Good. In the same way legal justice is termed a general virtue in that it directs the acts of all the virtues to the common good.

2. Sanctity seems to imply cleanness, for S. Denis says: "Sanctity is freedom from all impurity; it is perfect and stainless cleanness." Cleanness, however, seems to come under temperance, for this it is which precludes bodily defilement. Since, then, religion comes under justice, sanctity cannot be identified with religion.

Temperance indeed worketh cleanness, but this has not the ratio of sanctity except it be referred to God. Hence S. Augustine says of virginity itself that "not because it is virginity is it held in honour, but because it is consecrated to God."

3. Lastly, things that are contradistinguished are not identical. But in all enumerations of the parts of justice sanctity is set against religion.

But sanctity is set against religion because of the difference aforesaid; they differ indeed in idea, not in substance.

Cajetan: Religion is directly concerned with those things which specially pertain to the Divine worship—ceremonies, for example, sacrifices, oblations, etc. Whereas sanctity directly regards the mind, and through the mind the other virtuous works, including those of religion ... for it makes use of them so as thereby to apply the mind—and by consequence all acts that proceed from the human mind—to God. Thus we see that many religious people are not saints, whereas all saints are religious. For people who devote themselves to ceremonies, sacrifices, etc., can be termed religious; but they can only be called saints in so far as by means of these things they give themselves interiorly to God (*on* 2. 2. 81. 8).

QUESTION LXXXII

OF DEVOTION

1

Is Devotion a Special Kind of Act?

It is by our acts that we merit. But devotion has a peculiarly meritorious character. Consequently devotion is a special kind of act.

Devotion is so termed from "devoting" oneself. Hence the "devout" are so named because they "devote" themselves to God and thus proclaim their complete subjection to Him. Thus, too, among the heathen of old those were termed "devout" who for the army's sake "devoted" themselves to their idols unto death, as Livy tells us was the case with the two Decii. Hence devotion seems to mean nothing else than "the will to give oneself promptly to those things which pertain to God's service"; thus it is said in Exodus: *The multitude of the children of Israel ... offered first-fruits to the Lord with a most ready and devout mind.* It is clear, however, that a wish to do *readily* what belongs to God's service is a special act. Hence devotion is a special act of the will.

But some argue that devotion is not a special kind of act, thus:

1. That which serves to qualify other acts cannot be itself a special act. But devotion appears to qualify certain other acts; thus it is said that *all the multitude offered victims, and praises, and holocausts with a devout mind.*

But that which moves another gives a certain measure to the latter's movement. The will, however, moves the other faculties of the soul to their respective acts; and, moreover, the will, as aiming at an end in view, moves itself to the means towards that end. Consequently, since devotion is the act of a man who offers himself to serve Him Who is the Ultimate End, it follows that devotion gives a certain measure to human acts—whether they be the acts of the will itself with regard to the means to an end, or the acts of the other faculties as moved by the will.

2. Again, no act which finds a place in different kinds of acts can be itself a special kind of act. But devotion is to be found in acts of different kinds, both in corporal acts, for example, and in spiritual; thus a man is said to meditate devoutly, for instance, or to genuflect devoutly.

But devotion does not find a place in different kinds of acts as though it were a *species* coming under different *genera*, but in the same sense as the motive power of a moving principle is virtually discoverable in the movements of the things it sets in motion.

3. Lastly, all special kinds of acts belong either to the appetitive or to the cognoscitive faculties. But devotion comes under neither of these—as will be evident to anyone who will reflect upon the various acts of these faculties respectively.

But devotion is an act of the appetitive powers of the soul, and is, as we have said above, a movement of the will.

Cajetan: With regard to the proper meaning of the term *devotion*, note that since *devotion* is clearly derived from *devoting*, and since *to devote*—derived in its turn from *to vow*—means to promise something spontaneously to God: it follows that the principle in all such promises is the will; and further, not the will simply as such, but the will so affected as to be prompt. Hence in Latin those are said to be *devoted* to some superior whose will is so affected towards him as to make them prompt in his regard. And this seems to refer especially to God and to those who in a sense stand in His place, as, for instance, our rulers, our fatherland, and our principles of action. Hence in the Church's usage the term *devotion* is especially applied to those who are so affected towards God as to be prompt in His regard and in all that concerns Him. And so *devotion* is here taken to signify the act of a will so disposed, the act by which a man shows himself prompt in the Divine service.... Thus, then, *devotion*, the principal act of the virtue of religion, implies first of all the prompt desire of the Divine honour in our exercise of Divine worship; and hence comes the prompt choice of appropriate means to this end, and also the prompt carrying out of what we see to be suitable to that end. And the proof of possession of such *devotion* is that truly devout souls, the moment they perceive that some particular thing (or other) ought to be done for the service of God, are so promptly moved towards it that they rejoice in having to do or in actually doing it (*on* 2. 2. 82. 1).

S. Augustine: Give me, O Lord, Thyself; grant Thyself to me! For Thee do I love, and if my love be but weak, then would I love Thee more. For I cannot measure it so as to know how much my love falls short of that love which shall make my life run to Thy embraces nor ever turn away from Thee till I be hid in the hiding-place of Thy countenance. This only do I know: that it fares ill with me when away from Thee; and this not merely externally, but within me; for all abundance which is not my God is but penury for me! (*Confessions*, XIII. viii. 2).

II

Is Devotion an Act of the Virtue of Religion?

Devotion is derived from "devoting oneself" or making vows. But a vow is an act of the virtue of religion. Consequently devotion also is an act of the virtue of religion.

It belongs to the same virtue to wish to do a thing and to have a prompt will to do it, for the object of each of these acts is the same. For this reason the Philosopher says: "Justice is that by which men will and perform just deeds." And it is clear that to perform those things which pertain to the Divine worship or service comes under the virtue of religion. Consequently it belongs to the same virtue of religion to have a prompt will to carry out these things—in other words, to be devout. Whence it follows that devotion is an act of the virtue of religion.

But some argue that devotion is not an act of the virtue of religion, thus:

14

1. Devotion means that a man gives himself to God. But this belongs to the virtue of charity, for, as S. Denis says: "Divine love causes ecstasy since it permits not that those who love should belong any more to themselves, but to those things which they love." Whence devotion would seem to be rather an act of charity than of the virtue of religion.

It is indeed through charity that a man gives himself to God, clinging to Him by a certain union of soul; but that a man should give himself to God and occupy himself with the Divine service, is due directly to the virtue of religion, though indirectly it is due to the virtue of charity, which is the principle of the virtue of religion.

2. Again, charity precedes the virtue of religion. But devotion seems to precede charity; for charity is signified in Scripture by fire, and devotion by the fat of the sacrifices—the material on which the fire feeds. Consequently devotion is not an act of the virtue of religion.

But while the fat of the body is generated by the natural digestive heat, that natural heat finds its nourishment in that same fat. Similarly charity both causes devotion—since it is by love that a man becomes prompt to serve his friend—and at the same time charity is fed by devotion; just as all friendship is preserved and increased by the practice of friendly acts and by meditating upon them.

3. Lastly, by the virtue of religion a man turns to God alone. But devotion extends to men as well; people, for instance, are said to be devoted to certain Saints, and servants are said to be devoted to their masters, as S. Leo says of the Jews, that being devoted to the Roman laws, they said: *We have no king but Cæsar.* Consequently devotion is not an act of the virtue of religion.

But the devotion which we have to the Saints of God, whether living or dead, does not stop at them, but passes on to God, since we venerate God in God's ministers. And the devotion which subjects have to their temporal masters is of a different kind altogether, just as the service of temporal masters differs from the service of the Divine Master.

III

Is Contemplation, that is Meditation, the Cause of Devotion?

In Ps. xxxviii. 4 it is said: *And in my meditation a fire shall flame out.* But spiritual fire causes devotion. Therefore meditation causes devotion.

The extrinsic and principal cause of devotion is God Himself; thus S. Ambrose says: "God calls those whom He deigns to call; and whom He wills to make religious He makes religious; and had He willed it He would have made the Samaritans devout instead of indevout."

But the intrinsic cause of devotion on our part is meditation or contemplation. For, as we have said, devotion is a certain act of the will by which a man gives himself promptly to the Divine service. All acts of the will, however, proceed from consideration, since the will's object is good understood. Hence S. Augustine says: "The will starts from the understanding." Meditation must, then, be the cause of devotion inasmuch as it is from meditation that a man conceives the idea of giving himself up to God.

And two considerations lead a man to do this: one is the consideration of the Divine Goodness and of His benefits, whence the words of the Psalmist: *But for me it is good to cling close to my God, to put my hope in the Lord God.* And this consideration begets love, which is the proximate cause of devotion. And the second is man's consideration of his own defects which compel him to lean upon God, according to the words: *I have lifted up mine eyes to the mountains, from whence help shall come to me; my help is from the Lord Who made Heaven and earth.* This latter consideration excludes all presumption which, by making him lean upon himself, might prevent a man from submitting himself to God.

Some, however, argue that contemplation or meditation is not the cause of devotion, thus:

1. No cause hinders its own effect. But subtle intellectual meditations often hinder devotion.

But it is the consideration of those things which naturally tend to excite love of God which begets devotion; consideration of things which do not come under this head, but rather distract the mind from it, are a hindrance to devotion.

2. Again, if contemplation were the real cause of devotion, it should follow that the higher the matter of our contemplation the greater the devotion it begot. But the opposite is the case. For it frequently happens that greater devotion is aroused by the contemplation of the Passion of Christ and of the other mysteries of His Sacred Humanity than by meditation upon the Divine excellences.

It is true that things which concern the Godhead are of themselves more calculated to excite in us love, and consequently devotion, since God is to be loved above all things; yet it is due to the weakness of the human mind that just as it needs to be led by the hand to the knowledge of Divine things, so also must it be lead to Divine love by means of the things of sense already known to it; and the chief of these things is the Humanity of Christ, as is said in the *Preface* of the Mass: *So that knowing God visibly in the flesh, we may thereby be carried away to the love of things invisible.* Consequently the things that have to do with Christ's Humanity lead us, as it were, by the hand and are thus especially suited to stir up devotion in us; though, none the less, devotion is principally concerned with the Divinity.

3. Lastly, if contemplation were the real cause of devotion, it ought to follow that those who are the more fitted for contemplation are also the more fitted for devotion; whereas the contrary is the case, for greater devotion is often found among simple folk and in the female sex, where contemplation is wanting.

But knowledge, as indeed anything which renders a person great, occasions a man to trust in Himself, and hence he does not wholly give himself to God. It is for this reason that knowledge and suchlike things are sometimes a hindrance to a man's devotion, whereas among women and simple folk devotion abounds by the suppression of all elation. But if a man will only perfectly subject to God his knowledge and any other perfection he may have, then his devotion will increase.

Cajetan: Note these two intrinsic causes of devotion: one, namely, which arises from meditation upon God and His benefits, the other from meditation on our own defects. Under the first head I must consider God's goodness, mercy, and kindness towards mankind and towards myself; the benefits, for instance, of creation according to His own Likeness, of Redemption, of Baptism, of His inspirations, of His invitations—whether directly or through the medium of others; His patient waiting till I do penance; His Holy Eucharist; His preserving me from so many perils both of body and soul; His care of me by means of His Angels; and His other individual benefits. Under the second head come all my faults and the punishments due to me, whether in the past or now in the present; my proneness to sin; my misuse of my own powers by habituating my thoughts and desires—as well as the inclinations of my other various faculties—to evil; my sojourning in a region far away from His Friendship and from His Divine conversation; my perverted affections which make me think far more of temporal than of spiritual advantages or disadvantages; my utter lack of virtue; the wounds of my ignorance, of my malice, of my weakness, of my concupiscence; the shackles on my hands and feet, on my good works, that is; the shackles, too, on my affections, so that I dwell amidst darkness and rottenness and bitterness, and shrink not from it! My deafness, too, to the inner voice of my Shepherd; and, what is far worse, that I have chosen God for my enemy and my adversary as often as I have chosen mortal sin, and that I have thus offered Him the grievous insult of refusing to have Him for my God, and choosing instead my belly, or money, or false delights—and called them my God!

Meditations such as these should be in daily use among spiritual and religious people, and for their sake they should put aside the "much-speaking" of vocal prayer, however much it may appeal to them. And it is of such meditations that devotion and, by consequence, other virtues, are begotten. And they who do not give themselves to this form of prayer at least once in the day cannot be called religious men or women, nor even spiritual people. There can be no effect without a cause, no end without means to it, no gaining the harbour on the island save by a voyage in a ship; and so there can be no real religion without repeated acts regarding its causes, the means to it, and the vehicle that is to bring us thither (*on* 2. 2. 82. 3).

Cajetan: Just as he who removes an obstacle is the occasion of the resulting effect—a man, for instance, who pulls down a pillar is the occasion of the resulting fall of what it supported, and a man who removes a water-dam is the occasion of the consequent flood—so in the same way have women and simple folk a cause of devotion within themselves, for they have not that obstacle which consists in self-confidence. And because God bestows His grace on those who put no obstacle to it, the Church therefore calls the female sex "devout." Hence we are not to find fault with the learned for their knowledge, nor are we to praise women for womanly weakness; but that abuse of knowledge which consists in self-exaltation is blameworthy, just as the right use of women's weakness in not being uplifted is praiseworthy (*on* 2. 2. 82. 3).

IV

Is Joy an Effect of Devotion?

In the Church's *Collect* for the Thursday after the Fourth Sunday of Lent we say: *May holy devotion fill with joy those whom the fast they have undertaken chastises.*

Of itself indeed, and primarily, devotion brings about a spiritual joy of the mind; but as an accidental result it causes sorrow. For, as we have said above, devotion arises from two considerations. Primarily it arises from the consideration of the Divine Goodness, and from this thought there necessarily follows gladness, in accordance with the words: *I remembered God and was delighted.* Yet, as it were accidentally, this consideration begets a certain sadness in those who do not as yet fully enjoy God: *My soul hath thirsted after the strong living God,* and he immediately adds: *My tears have been my bread.*

Secondarily, however, devotion arises from the consideration of our own defects, for we thus reflect upon that from which a man, by devout acts of the will, turns away, so as no longer to dwell in himself, but to subject himself to God.

And this consideration is the converse of the former: for of itself it tends to cause sadness since it makes us dwell upon our defects; accidentally, however, it causes joy, for it makes us think of the hope we have of God's assistance.

Hence joy of heart primarily and of itself follows from devotion; but secondarily and accidentally there results a sadness which is unto God.

Some, however, argue that joy is not an effect of devotion, thus:

1. Christ's Passion, as said before, is especially calculated to cause devotion. But from dwelling on it there follows a certain affliction of soul: *Remember my poverty ... the wormwood and the gall*—that is, the Sacred Passion; and then follows: *I will be mindful, and remember, and my soul shall languish within me.*

In meditation on the Passion of Christ there is food for sadness—viz., the thought of the sins of men, and to take these away Christ had need to suffer. But there is also food for joy—viz., the thought of God's merciful kindness towards us in providing us such a deliverance.

2. Again, devotion principally consists in the interior sacrifice of the heart: *A sacrifice to God is an afflicted spirit;* consequently affliction, rather than pleasure or joy, is the outcome of devotion.

But the soul which is on the one hand saddened because of its shortcomings in this present life, is on the other hand delighted at the thought of the goodness of God and of the hope of Divine assistance.

3. Lastly, S. Gregory of Nyssa says: "Just as laughter proceeds from joy, so are sorrow and groaning signs of sadness." But out of devotion some burst into tears.

Yet tears spring not from sadness alone, but also from a certain tenderness of feeling: and especially is this the case when we reflect on something that, while pleasant, has in it a certain admixture of sadness; thus men are wont to weep from loving affection when they recover their children or others dear to them whom they had thought lost. And it is in this sense that tears spring from devotion.

Cajetan: Notice the proof here afforded that those are not devout persons who are habitually sad and gloomy, and who cannot mingle with others without getting into difficulties or dissolving into tears. For devout folk are cheerful, and are full of joy in their souls; and this not solely by reason of the principal cause, as is stated in the text, but also by reason of a secondary cause—the thought, namely, of their own failings. For the sadness of devout folk is *according to God*, and joy accompanies it; whence S. Augustine's remark: "Let a man grieve, but let him rejoice at his grief." Therefore it is that we read of the Saints that they were joyful and bright; and rightly so, for they had begun upon earth their "heavenly conversation" (*on* 2. 2. 82. 4).

S. Augustine: For Thee do I yearn, Justice and Innocence, Beautiful and Fair in Thy beauteous light that satisfies and yet never sates! For with Thee is repose exceedingly and life without disquiet! He that enters into Thee enters into the joy of his Lord; he shall know no fear, and in the Best shall be best. But I have deserted Thee and have wandered away, O Lord, my God! Too far have I wandered from Thee, the Steadfast One, in my youth, and I have become to myself a very land of want! (*Confessions*, II. x.).

QUESTION LXXXIII

OF PRAYER

I

Is Prayer an Act of the Appetitive Powers?

S. Isidore says: "To pray is the same thing as to speak." Speaking, however, belongs to the intellect. Hence prayer is not an act of the appetitive, but of the intellectual faculties.

According to Cassiodorus, on those words of the Psalmist: *Hear my prayer, O Lord, and my supplication, give ear to my tears,* prayer means "the lips' reasoning." Now there is this difference between the speculative and the practical reason, that the speculative reason merely apprehends things, while the practical reason not only apprehends things, but actually causes them. But one thing is the cause of another in two ways: in one way, perfectly—namely, as inducing a necessity—as happens when the effect comes entirely under the power of a cause; in another way, imperfectly—namely, by merely disposing to it—as happens when an effect is not entirely under the power of a cause.

And so, too, reason is in two ways the cause of certain things: in one way as imposing a necessity; and in this way it belongs to the reason to command not merely the lower faculties and the bodily members, but even men who are subject to us, and this is done by giving commands. In another way as inducing, and in some sort disposing to, an effect; and in this way the reason asks for something to be done by those who are subject to it, whether they be equals or superiors.

But both of these—namely, to command something, or to ask or beg for something to be done—imply a certain arrangement—as when a man arranges for something to be done by somebody else. And in this respect both of these acts come under the reason whose office it is to arrange. Hence the Philosopher says: "Reason asks for the best things."

Here, then, we speak of prayer as implying a certain asking or petition, for, as S. Augustine says: "Prayer is a certain kind of petition"; so, too, S. John Damascene says: "Prayer is the asking of fitting things from God."

Hence it is clear that the prayer of which we are here speaking is an act of the reason.

Some, however, think that prayer is an act of the appetitive powers, thus:

1. The whole object of prayer is to be heard, and the Psalmist says that it is our desires which are heard: *The Lord hath heard the desire of the poor.* Prayer, then, is desire; but desire is an act of the appetitive powers.

But the Lord is said to hear the desires of the poor either because their desire is the reason why they ask—since our petitions are in a certain sense the outward expression of our desires;

21

or this may be said in order to show the swiftness with which He hears them—even while things are only existing in the poor man's desire; God hears them even before they are expressed in prayer. And this accords with the words of Isaias: *And it shall come to pass that before they shall call I will hear, as they are yet speaking I will hear.*

2. Again, Denis the Areopagite says: "But before all things it is good to begin with prayer, as thereby giving ourselves up to and uniting ourselves with God." But union with God comes through love, and love belongs to the appetitive powers; therefore prayer, too, would seem to belong to the appetitive powers.

But the will moves the reason to its end or object. Hence there is nothing to prevent the reason, under the direction of the will, from tending to the goal of charity, which is union with God. Prayer, however, tends towards God—moved, that is, by the will, which itself is motived by charity—in two ways: in one way by reason of that which is asked for, since in prayer we have particularly to ask that we may be united with God, according to those words: *One thing I have asked of the Lord, this will I seek after, that I may dwell in the house of the Lord all the days of my life.* And in another way prayer tends towards God—by reason, namely, of the petitioner himself; for such a one must approach him from whom he asks something, and this either bodily, as when he draws nigh to a man, or mentally, as when he draws nigh to God.

Hence the same Denis says: "When we invoke God in prayer we are before Him with our minds laid bare." In the same sense S. John Damascene says: "Prayer is the ascent of the mind towards God." *Cajetan:* Prayer demands of the petitioner a twofold union with God: the one is general—the union, that is, of friendship—and is produced by charity, so that further on we shall find the friendship arising from charity enumerated among the conditions for infallibly efficacious prayer. The second kind of union may be termed substantial union; it is the effect of prayer itself. It is that union of application by which the mind offers itself and all it has to God in service—viz., by devout affections, by meditations, and by external acts. By such union as this a man who prays is inseparable from God in his worship and service, just as when one man serves another he is inseparable from him in his service (*on* 2. 2. 83. 1).

"And now, O Lord, Thou art our Father, and we are clay: and Thou art our Maker, and we are all the works of Thy hands. Be not very angry, O Lord, and remember no longer our iniquity: behold, see we are all Thy people."

II

Is It Fitting To Pray?

In S. Luke's Gospel we read: *We ought always to pray and not to faint.*

A threefold error regarding prayer existed amongst the ancients; for some maintained that human affairs were not directed by Divine Providence; whence it followed that it was altogether vain to pray or to worship God; of such we read: *You have said, he laboureth in vain that serveth God.* A second opinion was that all things, even human affairs, happened of necessity—whether from the immutability of Divine Providence, or from a necessity imposed by the stars, or from the connection of causes; and this opinion, of course, excluded all utility from prayer. A third opinion was that human affairs were indeed directed by Divine Providence, and that human affairs did not happen of necessity, but that Divine Providence was changeable, and that consequently its dispositions were changed by our prayers and by other acts of religious worship. These views, however, have elsewhere been shown to be wrong.

Consequently we have so to set forth the utility of prayer as neither to make things happen of necessity because subject to Divine Providence, nor to suggest that the arrangements of Divine Providence are subject to change.

To bring this out clearly we must consider that Divine Providence not merely arranges what effects shall take place, but also from what causes they shall proceed, and in what order.

But amongst other causes human acts are causes of certain effects. Hence men must do certain things, not so that their acts may change the Divine arrangement, but that by their acts they may bring about certain effects according to the order arranged by God; and it is the same with natural causes. It is the same, too, in the case of prayer. For we do not pray in order to change the Divine arrangements, but in order to win that which God arranged should be fulfilled by means of prayers; or, in S. Gregory's words: "Men by petitioning may merit to receive what Almighty God arranged before the ages to give them."

Some, however, maintain that prayer is futile, thus:

1. Prayer seems to be necessary in order that we may bring our wants to the notice of Him to Whom we make the petition. But our Lord says: *Your Father knoweth that ye have need of all these things.*

But it is not necessary for us to set forth our petitions before God in order to make known to Him our needs or desires, but rather that we ourselves may realize that in these things it is needful to have recourse to the Divine assistance.

2. Again, by prayer the mind of him to whom it is made is prevailed upon to grant what is asked of him; but the mind of God is unchangeable and inflexible: *The Triumpher in Israel will not spare, and will not be moved to repentance; for He is not a man that He should repent.* Consequently it is unavailing to pray to God.

But our prayers do not aim at changing the Divine arrangements, but at obtaining by our prayers what God has arranged to give us.

3. Lastly, it is more generous to give to one who does not ask than to one who asks, for, as Seneca remarks: "Nothing is bought at a dearer price than what is bought with prayers." Whereas God is most generous.

God, indeed, bestows on us many things out of His generosity, even things for which we do not ask; but He wishes to grant us some things on the supposition that we ask for them. And this is for our advantage, for it is intended to beget in us a certain confidence in having recourse to God, as well as to make us recognize that He is the Author of all good to us. Hence S. Chrysostom says: "Reflect what great happiness is bestowed upon you, what glory is given you, namely, to converse in your prayers with God, to join in colloquy with Christ, and to beg for what you wish or desire."

Cajetan: Notice how foolish are some Christians who, when desirous of reaching certain ends attainable by nature or art, are most careful to apply such means, and would rightly regard their hopes as vain unless they applied them; and yet at the same time they have quite false notions of the fruits to be derived from prayer: as though prayer were no cause at all, or at least but a remote one! Whence it comes to pass that, having false ideas about the causes, they fail to reap any fruit (*on* 2. 2. 83. 2).

S. Augustine: But some may say: It is not so much a question whether we are to pray by words or deeds as whether we are to pray at all if God already knows what is needful for us. Yet the very giving ourselves to prayer has the effect of soothing our minds and purifying them; it makes us more fit to receive the Divine gifts which are spiritually poured out upon us. For God does not hear us because of a display of prayer on our part; He is always ready, indeed, to give us His light, not, indeed, His visible light, but the light of the intellect and the spirit. It is we who are not always prepared to receive it, and this because we are preoccupied with other things and swallowed up in the darkness resulting from desire of the things of earth. When we pray, then, our hearts must turn to God, Who is ever ready to give if only we will take what He gives. And in so turning to Him we must purify the eye of our mind by shutting out all thought for the things of time, that so—with single-minded gaze—we may be able to bear that simple light that shines divinely, and neither sets nor changes. And not merely to bear it, but even to abide in it; and this not simply without strain, but with a certain unspeakable joy. In this joy the life of the Blessed is truly and really perfected (*On the Sermon on the Mount,* II. iii. 14).

S. Augustine: He could have bestowed these things on us even without our prayers; but He wished that by our prayers we should be taught from Whom these benefits come. For from whom do we receive them if not from Him from Whom we are bidden to ask them? Assuredly in this matter the Church does not demand laborious disputations; but note Her daily prayers: She prays that unbelievers may believe: God then brings them to the Faith. She prays that the faithful may persevere: God gives them perseverance to the end. And God foreknew that He would do these things. For this is the predestination of the Saints whom *He chose in Christ before the foundation of the world* (*Of the Gift of Perseverance,* vii. 15).

"Thou hast taught me, O God, from my youth; and till now I will declare Thy wonderful works. And unto old age and grey hairs, O God, forsake me not, until I shew forth Thy arm to all the generation that is to come."

III

Is Prayer an Act of the Virtue of Religion?

In Ps. cxl. 2 we read: *Let my prayer be directed as incense in Thy sight*, and on these words the Gloss remarks: "According to this figure, in the Old Law incense was said to be offered as an odour of sweetness to the Lord." And this comes under the virtue of religion. Therefore prayer is an act of religion.

It properly belongs to the virtue of religion to give due reverence and honour to God, and hence all those things by which such reverence is shown to God come under religion. By prayer, however, a man shows reverence to God inasmuch as he submits himself to Him and, by praying, acknowledges that he needs God as the Author of all his good. Whence it is clear that prayer is properly an act of religion.

Some, however, maintain that prayer is not an act of the virtue of religion, thus:

1. Prayer is rather the exercise of the Gift of Understanding than of the virtue of religion. For the virtue of religion comes under Justice; it is therefore resident in the will. But prayer belongs to the intellectual faculties, as we have shown above.

But we must remember that the will moves the other faculties of the soul to their objects or ends, and that consequently the virtue of religion, which is in the will, directs the acts of the other faculties in the reverence they show towards God. Now amongst these other faculties of the soul the intellect is the noblest and the most nigh to the will; consequently, next to devotion, which belongs to the will itself, prayer, which belongs to the intellective part, is the chief act of religion, for by it religion moves a man's understanding towards God.

2. Again, acts of worship fall under precept, whereas prayer seems to fall under no precept, but to proceed simply from the mere wish to pray; for prayer is merely asking for what we want; consequently prayer is not an act of the virtue of religion.

Yet not only to ask for what we desire, but to desire rightly, falls under precept; to desire, indeed, falls under the precept of charity, but to ask falls under the precept of religion—the precept which is laid down in the words: *Ask and ye shall receive.*

3. Lastly, the virtue of religion embraces due worship and ceremonial offered to the Divinity; prayer, however, offers God nothing, but only seeks to obtain things from Him.

In prayer a man offers to God his mind, which he subjects to Him in reverence, and which he, in some sort, lays bare before Him—as we have just seen in S. Denis's words. Hence, since the human mind is superior to all the other exterior or bodily members, and also to all exterior things which have place in the Divine worship, it follows that prayer, too, is pre-eminent among the acts of the virtue of religion.

Cajetan: In prayer or petition there are three things to be considered: the thing petitioned for, the actual petition, and the petitioner. As far, then, as the thing petitioned for is concerned, we give nothing to God when we pray; rather we ask Him to give us something. But if we consider the actual petition, then we do offer something to God when we pray. For the very act of petitioning is an act of subjection; it is an acknowledgment of God's power. And the proof of this is that proud men would prefer to submit to want rather than humble themselves by asking anything of others. Further, the petitioner, by the very fact that he petitions, acknowledges that he whom he petitions has the power to assist him, and is merciful, or just, or provident; it is for this reason that he hopes to be heard. Hence petition or prayer is regarded as an act of the virtue of religion, the object of which is to give honour to God. For we honour God by asking things of Him, and this by so much the more as—whether from our manner of asking or from the nature of what we ask for—we acknowledge Him to be above all things, to be our Creator, our Provider, our Redeemer, etc. And this is what S. Thomas points out in the body of the Article. But if we consider the petitioner: then, since man petitions with his mind—for petition is an act of the mind—and since the mind is the noblest thing in man, it follows that by petitioning we submit to God that which is noblest in us, since we use it to ask things of Him, and thereby do Him honour. Thus by prayer we offer our minds in sacrifice to God; so, too, by bending the knee to Him we offer to Him and sacrifice to Him our knees, by using them to His honour (*on* 2. 2. 83. 3).

S. Augustine: I stand as a beggar at the gate, He sleepeth not on Whom I call! Oh, may He give me those three loaves! For you remember the Gospel? Ah! see how good a thing it is to know God's word; those of you who have read it are stirred within yourselves! For you remember how a needy man came to his friend's house and asked for three loaves. And He says that he sleepily replied to him: "I am resting, and my children are with me asleep." But he persevered in his request, and wrung from him by his importunity what his deserts could not get. But God wishes to give; yet only to those who ask—lest He should give to those who understand not. He does not wish to be stirred up by your weariness! For when you pray you are not being troublesome to one who sleeps; *He slumbereth not nor sleeps that keepeth Israel.* ... He, then, sleeps not; see you that your faith sleeps not! (*Enarr. in Ps.* cii. 10).

S. Augustine: Some there are who either do not pray at all, or pray but tepidly; and this because, forsooth, they have learnt from the Lord Himself that God knows, even before we ask Him, what is necessary for us. But because of such folk are we to say that these words are not true and therefore to be blotted out of the Gospel? Nay, rather, since it is clear that God gives some things even to those who do not ask—as, for instance, the beginnings of faith—and has prepared other things for those only who pray for them—as, for instance, final perseverance—it is evident that he who fancies he has this latter of himself does not pray to have it (*Of the Gift of Perseverance*, xvi. 39).

"I will sing to the Lord as long as I live; I will sing praise to my God while I have my being. Let my speech be acceptable to Him; but I will take delight in the Lord."

IV

Ought We To Pray To God Alone?

In Job v. 1 we read: *Call, now, if there be any that will answer thee, and turn to some of the Saints.*

Prayer is addressed to a person in two ways: in one way as a petition to be granted by him; in another way as a petition to be forwarded by him. In the former way we only pray to God, for all our prayers ought to be directed to the attaining of grace and glory, and these God alone gives: *The Lord will give grace and glory.* But in the latter way we set forth our prayers both to the holy Angels and to men; and this, not that through their intervention God may know our petitions, but rather that by their prayers and merits our petitions may gain their end. Hence it is said in the Apocalypse: *And the smoke of the incense of the prayers of the Saints ascended up before God from the hand of the Angel.* And this is clearly shown, too, from the style adopted by the Church in her prayers: for of the Holy Trinity we pray that mercy may be shown us; but of all the Saints, whomsoever they may be, we pray that they may intercede for us.

Some, however, maintain that we ought to pray to God alone, thus:

1. Prayer is an act of the virtue of religion. But only God is to be worshipped by the virtue of religion. Consequently it is to Him alone that we should pray.

But in our prayers we only show religious worship to Him from Whom we hope to obtain what we ask, for by so doing we confess Him to be the Author of all our goods; but we do not show religious worship to those whom we seek to have as intercessors with us before God.

2. Again, prayer to those who cannot know what we pray for is idle. But God alone can know our prayers, and this because prayer is frequently a purely interior act of which God alone is cognizant, as the Apostle says: *I will pray with the spirit. I will pray also with the understanding*; and also because, as S. Augustine says: The dead know not, not even the Saints, what the living—not even excepting their own children—are doing.

It is true that the dead, if we consider only their natural condition, do not know what is done on earth, and especially do they not know the interior movements of the heart. But to the Blessed, as S. Gregory says, manifestation is made in the Divine Word of those things which it is fitting that they should know as taking place in our regard, even the interior movements of the heart. And, indeed, it is most befitting their state of excellence that they should be

27

cognizant of petitions addressed to them, whether vocally or mentally. Hence through God's revelation they are cognizant of the petitions which we address them.

3. Lastly, some say: if we do address prayers to any of the Saints, the sole reason for doing so lies in the fact that they are closely united to God. But we do not address prayers to people who, while still living in this world, are closely knit to God, nor to those who are in Purgatory and are united to Him. There seems, then, to be no reason why we should address prayers to the Saints in Paradise. But they who are still in the world or in Purgatory do not as yet enjoy the vision of the Divine Word so as to be able to know what we think or say, hence we do not implore their help when we pray; though when talking with living people we do ask them to help us.

S. Augustine: It is no great thing to live long, nor even to live for ever; but it is indeed a great thing to live well. Oh, let us love eternal life! And we realize how earnestly we ought to strive for that eternal life when we note how men who love this present temporal life so work for it—though it is to pass away—that, when the fear of death comes, they strive all they can, not, indeed, to do away with death, but to put death off! How men labour when death approaches! They flee from it; they hide from it; they give all they have; they try to buy themselves off; they work and strive; they put up with tortures and inconveniences; they call in physicians; they do everything that lies within their power! Yet even if they spend all their toil and their substance, they can only secure that they may live a little longer, not that they may live for ever! If, then, men spend such toil, such endeavour, so much money, so much anxiety, watchfulness, and care, in order to live only a little longer, what ought we not to do that we may live for ever? And if we call them prudent who take every possible precaution to stave off death, to live but a few days more, to save just a few days, then how foolish are they who so pass their days as to lose the Day of Eternity! (*Sermon,* cxxvii. 2).

"May God have mercy on us, and bless us: may He cause the light of His countenance to shine upon us, and may He have mercy on us. That we may know Thy way upon earth: Thy salvation in all nations. Let people confess to Thee, O God: let all people give praise to Thee. Let the nations be glad and rejoice: for Thou judgest the people with justice, and directest the nations upon earth. Let the people, O God, confess to Thee: let all the people give praise to Thee: the earth hath yielded her fruit. May God, our God bless us, may God bless us: and all the ends of the earth fear Him."

V

Should We in our Prayers ask for Anything Definite from God?

Our Lord taught the disciples to ask definitely for the things which are contained in the petitions of the Lord's Prayer: *Thus shalt thou pray.*

Maximus Valerius tells of Socrates that he "maintained that nothing further should be asked of the immortal gods save that they should give us good things; and this on the ground that they knew well what was best for each individual, whereas we often ask in our prayers for things which it would be better not to have asked for." And this opinion has some truth in it as regards those things which can turn out ill, or which a man can use well or ill, as, for example, riches which, as the same Socrates says, "have been to the destruction of many; or honours which have ruined many; or the possession of kingdoms, the issues of which are so often ill-fated; or splendid matrimonial alliances, which have sometimes proved the ruin of families." But there are certain good things of which a man cannot make a bad use—those, namely, which cannot have a bad issue. And these are the things by which we are rendered blessed and by which we merit beatitude; these are the things for which the Saints pray unconditionally: *Show us Thy Face and we shall be saved*; and again: *Lead me along the path of Thy commandments.*

Some, however, say that we ought not in our prayers to ask for definite things from God, thus:

1. S. John Damascene defines prayer as "asking from God things that are fitting"; consequently prayer for things which are not expedient is of no efficacy, as S. James says: *You ask and receive not, because you ask amiss.* Moreover, S. Paul says: *We know not what we should pray for as we ought.*

But it is also true that though a man cannot of himself know what he ought to pray for, yet, as the Apostle says in the same place: *In this the Spirit helpeth our infirmity*—namely, in that, by inspiring us with holy desires, He makes us ask aright. Hence Our Lord says that the true adorers *must adore in spirit and in truth.*

2. Further, he who asks from another some definite thing strives to bend that other's will to do what the petitioner wants. But we ought not to direct our prayers towards making God will what we will, but rather we should will what He wills—as the Gloss says on the words of Ps. xxxii. 1: *Rejoice in the Lord, O ye just!* It would seem, therefore, that we ought not to ask for definite things from God when we pray.

Yet when in our prayers we ask for things which appertain to our salvation, we are conforming our will to the will of God, for of His will it is said: *He will have all men to be saved.*

3. Lastly, evil things cannot be asked from God; and He Himself invites us to receive good things. But it is idle for a person to ask for what he is invited to receive.

God, it is true, invites us to receive good things; but He wishes us to come to them—not, indeed, by the footsteps of the body—but by pious desires and devout prayers.

S. Augustine: Fly, then, by unwavering faith and holy habits, fly, brethren, from those torments where the torturers never desist, and where the tortured never die; whose death is unending, and where in their anguish they cannot die. But burn with love for and desire of the eternal life of the Saints where there is no longer the life of toil nor yet wearisome repose. For the praises of God will beget no disgust, neither will they ever cease. There will there be no weariness of the soul, no bodily fatigue; there will there be no wants: neither wants of your own which will call for succour, nor wants of your neighbour demanding your speedy help. God will be all your delight; there will ye find the abundance of that Holy City that from Him draws life and happily and wisely lives in Him. For there, according to that promise of His for which we hope and wait, we shall be made equal to the Angels of God; and equally with them shall we then enjoy that vision of the Holy Trinity in which we now but walk by faith. For we now believe what we do not see, that so by the merits of that same faith we then may merit to see what we believe, and may so hold fast to it that the Equality of Father, Son, and Holy Ghost, and the Unity of the Trinity, may no longer come to us under the garb of faith, nor be the subject of contentious talk, but may rather be what we may drink in in purest and deepest contemplation amid the silence of Eternity (*De Catechizandis Rudibus*, xxv. 47).

S. Augustine: O Lord, my God, give me what Thou biddest and then bid what Thou wilt! Thou biddest us be continent. *And I knew*, as a certain one says, *that I could not otherwise be continent save God gave it, and this also was a point of wisdom to know Whose gift it was.* Now by continence we are knit together and brought back into union with that One from Whom we have wandered away after many things. For he loves Thee but little who loves other things with Thee, and loves them not for Thee! O Love that ever burnest and wilt never be extinguished! O Charity! O Lord, my God, set me on fire! Thou dost bid continence? Then give me what Thou biddest and bid what Thou wilt! (*Confessions*, X. xxix.).

S. Augustine: O Lord, my God, listen to my prayer and mercifully hear my desire! For my desire burns not for myself alone, but fraternal charity bids it be of use. And Thou seest in my heart that it is so; for I would offer to Thee in sacrifice the service of my thoughts and of my tongue. Grant me then what I may offer to Thee. For I am needy and poor, and Thou art rich towards all that call upon Thee; for in peace and tranquillity hast Thou care for us. Circumcise, then, my lips, within and without, from all rashness and all untruthfulness. May Thy Scriptures be my chaste delight; may I never be deceived in them nor deceive others out of them. Attend, O Lord, and have mercy upon me, O Lord, my God. Thou art the Light of the blind, the Strength of the weak, and so, too, art Thou the Light of them that see and the Strength of them that are strong. Look, then, on my soul, and hear me when I cry from out the depths! (*Confessions*, XI. ii. 2).

"Look down from Heaven, and behold from Thy holy habitation and the place of Thy glory: where is Thy zeal, and Thy strength, the multitude of Thy bowels, and of Thy mercies? they have held back themselves from me. For Thou art our Father, and Abraham hath not known us, and Israel hath been ignorant of us: Thou, O Lord, art our Father, our Redeemer, from everlasting is Thy Name."

VI

Ought We in our Prayers to ask for Temporal Things from God?

We have the authority of the Book of Proverbs for answering in the affirmative, for there we read: *Give me only the necessaries of life.*

S. Augustine says to Proba: "It is lawful to pray for what it is lawful to desire." But it is lawful to desire temporal things, not indeed as our principal aim or as something which we make our end, but rather as props and stays which may be of assistance to us in our striving for the possession of God; for by such things our bodily life is sustained, and such things, as the Philosopher says, co-operate organically to the production of virtuous acts. Consequently it is lawful to pray for temporal things. And this is what S. Augustine means when he says to Proba: "Not unfittingly does a person desire sufficiency for this life when he desires it and nothing more; for such sufficiency is not sought for its own sake but for the body's health, and for a mode of life suitable to a man's position so that he may not be a source of inconvenience to those with whom he lives. When, then, we have these things we must pray that we may retain them, and when we have not got them we must pray that we may have them."

Some, however, argue that we ought not to pray for temporal things, thus:

1. What we pray for we seek. But we are forbidden to seek for temporal things, for it is said: *Seek ye therefore first the kingdom of God, and His justice, and all these things shall be added unto you*, those temporal things, namely, which He says are not to be sought but which are to be added to the things which we seek.

But temporal things are to be sought secondarily not primarily. Hence S. Augustine: "When He says the former is *to be sought first* (namely the kingdom of God), He means that the latter (namely temporal good things) are to be sought afterwards; not *afterwards* in point of time, but *afterwards* in point of importance; the former as our good, the latter as our need."

2. Again, we only ask for things about which we are solicitous. But we are not allowed to be solicitous about temporal concerns: *Be not solicitous for your life, what ye shall eat....*

But not all solicitude about temporal affairs is forbidden, only such as is superfluous and out of due order.

3. Further, we ought in prayer to uplift our minds to God. But by asking for temporal things in prayer our mind descends to things beneath it, and this is contrary to the teaching of the Apostle: *While we look not at the things which are seen, but at the things which are not seen. For the things which are seen are temporal: but the things which are not seen are eternal.*

31

When our mind is occupied with temporal affairs so as to set up its rest in them then it remains in them, and is depressed by them; but when the mind turns to them as a means of attaining to eternal life it is not depressed by them, but rather uplifted by them.

4. Lastly, men ought not to pray except for things useful and good. But temporal possessions are at times hurtful, and this not merely spiritually but even temporally; hence a man ought not to ask them of God.

But it is clear that since we do not seek temporal things primarily or for their own sake, but with reference to something else, we consequently only ask them of God according as they may be expedient for our salvation.

S. Augustine: *Lord, all my desire is before Thee, and my groaning is not hid from Thee!* It is not before men who cannot see the heart, but *before Thee is all my desire.* And let your desires, too, be before Him, and your Father Who seeth in secret will repay thee. For your very desire is a prayer, and if your desire is continual your prayer, too, is continual. Not without reason did the Apostle say: *Pray without ceasing.* Yet can we genuflect without ceasing? Can we prostrate without ceasing? Can we lift up our hands without ceasing? How, then, does he say: *Pray without ceasing?* If by *prayer* he meant such things as these then I think we could not pray without ceasing. But there is another prayer, an interior prayer, which is without ceasing—*desire.* Whatever else you do, if only you desire that *rest* you cease not to pray. If you wish to pray without ceasing then desire without ceasing. Your continual desire is your continual voice; but you will be silent if you cease to love (*Enarr. in Ps.* xxxvii. 10).

S. Augustine: But all these things are the gifts of my God; I did not give them to myself; they are good, and all these things am I. He then is good Who made me; nay, He Himself is my Good, and in Him do I rejoice for all the good things which I had even as a boy! But in this did I sin that, not in Him but in His creatures did I seek myself and other pleasures, high thoughts and truths. Thus it was that I fell into sorrow, confusion, and error. Thanks be to Thee, my Sweetness, my Honour and my Trust, O my God! Thanks be to Thee for Thy gifts! But do Thou keep them for me! For so doing Thou wilt be keeping me, and those things which Thou hast given me will be increased and perfected, and I myself shall be with Thee, for even that I should be at all is Thy gift to me! (*Confessions,* I. xx. 2).

S. Augustine: But I forget not, neither will I keep silence regarding the severity of Thy scourge and the wondrous swiftness of Thy mercy. Thou didst torture me with toothache; and when the pain had become so great that I could not even speak, it came into my mind to tell all my friends who were there to pray to Thee for me, to Thee the God of all manner of succour. And I wrote my request on a wax tablet and I gave it them to read. And hardly had we bent the knee in humble prayer than the pain fled! But what a pain it was! And how did it disappear? I was terrified, I confess it, O Lord my God! Never in all my life had I felt anything like it! (*Confessions,* IX. iv. 12).

It is narrated of S. Thomas that when at Paris it happened that having to lecture at the University on a subject which he had commenced the day before, he rose at night to pray as was his wont, but discovered that a tooth had suddenly pushed its way through his gums in such a way that he could not speak. His companion suggested that since it was an inopportune time for procuring assistance a message should be sent to the University stating what had happened and pointing out that the lecture could not be given till the tooth had been removed by a surgeon. But S. Thomas, reflecting upon the difficulty in which the University would be placed, considering also the danger which might arise from the removal of the tooth in the way suggested, said to his companion: I see no remedy save to trust to God's Providence. He then betook himself to his accustomed place of prayer, and for a long space besought God with tears to grant him this favour, leaving himself entirely in His hands. And when he had thus prayed he took the tooth between his fingers, and it came out at once without the slightest pain or wrench, and he found himself freed from the impediment to his speech which it had caused. This tooth he carried about with him for a long time as a reminder of an act of Divine loving-kindness such as he was anxious not to forget, for forgetfulness is the mother of ingratitude; he wished it, too, to move him to still greater confidence in the power of prayer which had on that occasion been so quickly heard (see *Vita S. Thomæ*, Bollandists, March 7, vol. i., 1865, pp. 673, 704, 712).

S. Augustine: But temporal things are sometimes for our profit, sometimes for our hurt. For many poverty was good, wealth did them harm. For many a hidden life was best, high station did them harm. And on the other hand money was good for some, and dignities, too, were good for them—good, that is, for those who used them well; but such things did harm when not taken away from those who used them ill. Consequently, brethren, let us ask for these temporal things with moderation, being sure that if we do receive them, He gives them Who knoweth what is best suited to us. You have asked for something, then, and what you asked for has not been given you? Believe in your Father Who would give it you if it were expedient for you (*Sermon*, lxxx. 7).

S. Augustine: Sometimes God in His wrath grants what you ask; at other times in His mercy He refuses what you ask. When, then, you ask of Him things which He praises, which He commands, things which He has promised us in the next world, then ask in confidence and be instant in prayer as far as in you lies, that so you may receive what you ask. For such things as these are granted by the God of mercy; they flow not from His wrath but from His compassion. But when you ask for temporal things, then ask with moderation, ask with fear; leave all to Him so that if they be for your profit He may give them you, if they be to your hurt He may refuse them. For what is for our good and what is to our hurt the Physician knoweth, not the patient (*Sermon*, cccliv. 8).

"Cast thy care upon the Lord, and He shall sustain thee; He shall not suffer the just to waver for ever."

VII

Ought We To Pray for Others?

S. James, in his Epistle, says: *Pray for one another that ye may be saved.*

As we said above, we ought in prayer to ask for those things which we ought to desire. But we ought to desire good things not for ourselves only but also for others, for this belongs to that charity which we ought to exercise towards our neighbour. Hence charity demands that we pray for others. In accordance with this S. Chrysostom says: "Necessity compels us to pray for ourselves, fraternal charity urges us to pray for others. But that prayer is more pleasing before God which arises not so much from our needs as from the demands of fraternal charity."

Some, however, urge that we ought not to pray for others, thus:

1. We are bound in our prayer to follow the norm which our Lord delivered to us; but in the *Lord's Prayer* we pray for ourselves and not for others, for we say: *Give us this day our daily bread*, etc.

But S. Cyprian says: "We do not say *my* Father, but *our* Father, neither do we say Give *me*, but give *us*; and this because the Teacher of Unity did not wish prayer to be made privately, viz., that each should pray for himself alone; for He wished one to pray for all since He in His single Person had borne all."

2. Again, we pray in order to be heard; but one of the conditions for our prayer to be heard is that a man should pray for himself. Thus on the words: *If ye ask the Father anything in My Name He will give it you*, S. Augustine says: "All are heard for themselves, but not for all in general, hence He does not say simply: *He will give it*, but *He will give it you*."

But to pray for oneself is a condition attaching to prayer; not indeed a condition affecting its merit, but a condition which is necessary if we would ensure the attainment of what we ask. For it sometimes happens that prayer made for another does not avail even though it be devout and persevering and for things pertaining to a man's salvation; and this is because of the existence of some hindrance on the part of him for whom we pray, as we read in Jeremias: *If Moses and Samuel shall stand before Me, My soul is not towards this people.* None the less, such prayer will be meritorious on the part of him who prays, for he prays out of charity; thus on the words, *And my prayer shall be turned into my bosom*, the Interlinear Gloss has: "That is, and even though it avail not for them, yet shall I not be without my reward."

3. Lastly, we are forbidden to pray for others if they are wicked, according to the words: *Do not thou pray for this people ... and do not withstand Me, for I will not hear thee.* And, on the other hand, we ought not to pray for them if they are good, for in that case they will be heard when they pray for themselves.

But we have to pray even for sinners, that they may be converted, and for the good, that they may persevere and make progress. Our prayers for sinners, however, are not heard for all, but for some. For they are heard for those who are predestined, not for those who are foreknown as reprobate; just in the same way as when we correct our brethren, such corrections avail among the predestinate but not among the reprobate, according to the words: *No man can correct whom He hath despised.* Wherefore also it is said: *He that knoweth his brother to sin a sin that is not unto death, let him ask, and life shall be given to him who sinneth not to death.* But just as we can refuse to no one, as long as he liveth on this earth, the benefit of correction—for we cannot distinguish between the predestinate and the reprobate, as S. Augustine says—so neither can we refuse to anyone the suffrage of our prayers.

And for good men we have to pray, and this for a threefold reason: firstly, because the prayers of many are more easily heard; thus on the words: *I beseech ye therefore, help me in your prayers for me*, the Ordinary Gloss of S. Ambrose says: "Well does the Apostle ask his inferiors to pray for him; for even the very least become great when many in number, and when gathered together with one mind; and it is impossible that the prayers of many should not avail" to obtain, that is, what is obtainable. And secondly, that thanks may be returned by many for the benefits conferred by God upon the just, for these same benefits tend to the profit of many—as is evident from the Apostle's words to the Corinthians. And thirdly, that those who are greater may not therefore be proud, but may realize that they need the suffrages of their inferiors. "Father, I will that where I am they also whom Thou hast given Me may be with Me; that they may see My glory, which Thou hast given Me: because Thou hast loved Me before the foundation of the world."

VIII

Ought We To Pray for Our Enemies?

But I say to you ... pray for them that persecute and calumniate you.

To pray for others is a work of charity, as we have said above. Hence we are bound to pray for our enemies in the same way as we are bound to love them. We have already explained, in the *Treatise on Charity*, in what sense we are bound to love our enemies; namely, that we are bound to love their nature, not their fault; and that to love our enemies in general is of precept; to love them, however, individually, is not of precept save in the sense of being prepared to do so; a man, for instance, is bound to be ready to love an individual enemy and to help him in case of necessity, or if he comes to seek his pardon. But absolutely to love our individual enemies, and to assist them, belongs to perfection.

In the same way, then, it is necessary that in our general prayers for others we should not exclude our enemies. But to make special prayer for them belongs to perfection and is not necessary, save in some particular cases. Some, however, argue that we ought not to pray for our enemies, thus:

1. It is said in the Epistle to the Romans: *What things soever were written were written for our learning.* But in Holy Scripture we find many imprecations against enemies; thus, for instance: *Let all my enemies be ashamed, let them be turned back and be ashamed very speedily.* From which it would rather seem that we ought to pray against our enemies than for them.

But the imprecations which find place in Holy Scripture can be understood in four different ways: first of all according as the Prophets are wont "to predict the future under the figure of imprecations," as S. Augustine says; secondly, in that certain temporal evils are sometimes sent by God upon sinners for their amendment; thirdly, these denunciations may be understood, not as demanding the punishment of men themselves, but as directed against the kingdom of sin, in the sense that by men being corrected sin may be destroyed; fourthly, in that the Prophets conform their wills to the Divine Justice with regard to the damnation of sinners who persevere in their sin.

2. Further, to be revenged upon our enemies means evil for our enemies. But the Saints seek to be avenged upon their enemies: *How long, O Lord, dost Thou not judge and revenge our blood on them that dwell on the earth?* And in accordance with this we find them rejoicing in the vengeance taken upon sinners: *The just shall rejoice when he shall see the revenge.* It would seem, then, that we ought rather to pray against our enemies than for them.

But, on the contrary, as S. Augustine says: "The vengeance of the martyrs is the overthrow of the empire of sin under whose dominion they suffered so much"; or, as he says elsewhere: "They demand vengeance, not by word of mouth, but by very reason, just as the blood of Abel cried out from the earth." Moreover, they rejoice in this vengeance, not for its own sake, but because of the Divine Justice.

3. Lastly, a man's deeds and his prayers cannot be in opposition. But men sometimes quite lawfully attack their enemies, else all wars would be illegal. Hence we ought not to pray for our enemies.

But it is lawful to assail our enemies that so they may be hindered from sin; and this is for their good and for that of others. In the same way, then, it is lawful to pray for temporal evils for our enemies to the end that they may be corrected. In this sense our deeds and our prayers are not in opposition.

S. Augustine: If there were no wicked folk, then for whom could we be supposed to pray when we are told: *Pray for your enemies?* Perhaps you would like to have good enemies. Yet how could that be? For unless you yourself are bad you will not have good people for enemies; and if, on the contrary, you are good, then no one will be your enemy save the wicked folk (*Sermon,* xv., *on Ps.* xxv. 8).

"Have mercy upon us, O God of all, and behold us, and shew us the light of Thy mercies: And send Thy fear upon the nations, that have not sought after Thee: that they may know that there is no God beside Thee, and that they may shew forth Thy wonders. Lift up Thy hand over the strange nations, that they may see Thy power."

On the Seven Petitions of the *lord's Prayer*.

The Lord's Prayer is the most perfect of all prayers, for, as S. Augustine says to Proba: "If we pray rightly and fittingly we can say nothing else but what is set down in the *Lord's Prayer*." And since prayer is, in a sort, the interpreter of our desires before God, we can only rightly ask in prayer for those things which we can rightly desire. But in the *Lord's Prayer* not only do we have petitions for all those things which we can rightly desire, but they are set forth in the order in which they are to be desired. Hence this prayer not only teaches us how to pray, but serves as the norm of all our dispositions of mind.

For it is clear that we desire first the end and then the means to the attainment of that end. But our end is God, towards Whom our desires tend in two ways: first, in that we desire God's glory; secondly, in that we desire to enjoy that glory ourselves. The former of these pertains to that love wherewith we love God in Himself, the latter to that charity wherewith we love ourselves in God. Hence the first petition runs: *Hallowed be Thy Name*, wherein we pray for God's glory; and the second runs: *Thy kingdom come*, wherein we pray that we may come to the glory of His kingdom.

But to this said end things lead us in two ways: viz., either *essentially* or *accidentally*. Things which are useful for the attainment of that end *essentially* lead us to it. But a thing may be useful as regards that end which is the possession of God in two ways: namely, *directly and principally*, that is, according to the merits by which we merit the possession of God by obeying Him; and in accordance with this runs the petition: *Thy Will be done on earth as it is in Heaven*; also *instrumentally* as assisting us to merit, whence the petition: *Give us this day our daily bread*. And this is true whether we understand by this "bread" that Sacramental Bread, the daily use of Which profits man, and in Which are comprised all the other Sacraments; or whether we understand it of material bread so that "bread" here means all that is sufficient for the support of life—as S. Augustine explains it to Proba. For both the Holy Eucharist is the chief of Sacraments, and bread is the chief of foods, whence in the Gospel of S. Matthew we have the term "super-substantial" or "special" applied to it, as S. Jerome explains it.

And we are lead, as it were, *accidentally* to the possession of God by the removal of impediments from our path. Now there are three things which impede us in our efforts after the possession of God. The first of these is sin, which directly excludes us from the kingdom: *Neither fornicators, nor idolaters, ... etc., shall possess the kingdom of God*; hence the petition: *Forgive us our trespasses....* And the second impediment is temptation which hinders us from obeying the Divine Will; whence the petition: *And lead us not into temptation*; in which petition we do not pray that we may not be tempted, but that we may not be overcome by temptation, for this is the meaning of being led into temptation. And the third hindrance lies in our present penal state which prevents us from having "the sufficiency of life"; and for this reason we say: *Deliver us from evil.*

Some, however, argue that these seven petitions are not very appropriate, thus:

1. It seems idle to pray that that may be hallowed which is already hallowed or holy. But the Name of God is holy: *And holy is His Name.* Similarly, His kingdom is everlasting: *Thy kingdom, O Lord, is a kingdom of all ages.* God's Will, too, is always fulfilled: *And all My Will shall be done.* Hence it is idle to pray that God's Name may be hallowed, that His kingdom may come, and that His Will may be done.

But, as S. Augustine says, when we say, *Hallowed be Thy Name*, we do not make this petition as though God's Name were not holy, but that It may be held holy by men; in other words, that God's glory may be propagated amongst men. And when we say, *Thy kingdom come*, it is not as though we meant that God did not reign, but, as S. Augustine says to Proba: "We stir up our desires for that kingdom, that it may come upon us and that we may reign in it." Lastly, when we say, *Thy Will be done*, this is rightly understood to mean: May Thy precepts be obeyed *on earth as in Heaven*—that is, as by Angels, so by men. These three petitions, then, will receive their perfect fulfilment in the life to come; but the remaining four, as S. Augustine says, refer to the necessities of the present life.

2. But further, to depart from evil must precede the pursuit of what is good. Hence it hardly seems appropriate to place those petitions which are concerned with the pursuit of what is good before those which refer to the departing from evil.

Yet since prayer is the interpreter of our desires the order of these petitions does not correspond to the order of attainment but of desire or intention; in this order, however, the end precedes the means to the end, the pursuit of good comes before the departure from evil.

3. But once more, we ask for something in order that it may be given us. But the chief gift of God is the Holy Spirit and those things which are given us through Him. Hence these petitions do not seem to be very appropriate since they do not correspond to the Gifts of the Holy Spirit.

S. Augustine, however, adapts these seven petitions to the Gifts of the Holy Spirit and to the Beatitudes; he says: "If we have the *fear of God* by which the poor in spirit are blessed, we pray that God's Name may be hallowed among men by chaste fear. If we have *piety*, by which the meek are blessed, we pray that His kingdom may come, that we may be meek, and that we may not withstand It. If we have *knowledge*, by which they that mourn are blessed, we pray that His will may be done, and that so we may not mourn. If we have *fortitude*, by which they that hunger are blessed, we pray that our daily bread may be given us. If we have *counsel*, by which they that are merciful are blessed, let us forgive our debtors that we ourselves may be forgiven. If we have *understanding*, by which the clean of heart are blessed, let us pray that we may not have a double heart that pursues after temporal things whence temptations come to us. If we have *wisdom*, whence the peace-makers are blessed—for they shall be called the sons of God—let us pray that we may be delivered from evil, for that very deliverance will make us the free sons of God."

4. Again, according to S. Luke, there are only five petitions in the Lord's Prayer. Hence it would seem superfluous to have seven in S. Matthew.

But, as S. Augustine says: "S. Luke only includes five petitions and not seven in the Lord's Prayer, for he shows that the third petition is, in a sense, only a repetition of the two preceding ones; by omitting it he makes us see that God's will is more especially concerned with our knowledge of His sanctity and with our reigning with Him. But Luke has omitted Matthew's last petition, *Deliver us from evil*, in order to show us that we are delivered from evil just precisely as we are not led into temptation."

5. And lastly, it seems idle to try to stir up the benevolence of one who is beforehand with his benevolence. But God does forestall us with His benevolence, for *He hath first loved us*. Consequently it seems superfluous to preface our petitions with the words *Our Father Who art in Heaven*, words which seem intended to stir up God's benevolence.

But we must remember that prayer is not directed to God in order to prevail upon Him, but in order to excite ourselves to confidence in our petitions. And this confidence is especially excited in us by consideration of His love towards us whereby He wishes us well, wherefore we say, *Our Father*, and of His pre-eminent power whereby He is able to assist us, whence we say, *Who art in Heaven*.

Cajetan: The first three petitions of the *Lord's Prayer* can also be referred to that which we principally desire, so that all three regard mainly that love wherewith we love God in Himself, and secondarily that love wherewith we love ourselves in God. And the proof of this is that in each of the first three we have the pronoun *Thine*, but in the last four the pronoun *our*. Thus the first petition asks for the effective and enduring praise of God's Name; the second, that He—and not the devil, nor the world, nor the flesh, nor sin—may reign effectively; the third, that His Will may be effectively fulfilled. For these things are not now absolutely so with God, and this by reason of the multitude of sins, and also because the mode of their present fulfilment is hidden. And the word *effectively* is introduced into each clause by reason of the subjoined qualification *on earth as it is in Heaven*, for this qualifies each of the foregoing clauses. Hence rightly do our desires first of all aim at, wish for, and pray that—even as something good for God Himself—He may be sanctified in His Name; that He may be permanently uplifted above all things—on earth as in Heaven; that He—not sin—may reign—on earth as in Heaven; that His Will—none other—may be done—on earth as in Heaven (*on* 2. 2. 83. 9).

S. Augustine: O Eternal Truth, True Love and lovable Eternity! Thou art my God; for Thee do I sigh night and day! And when I first knew Thee Thou didst snatch me up so that I saw that That really was Which I saw, and that I who saw was really not—as yet. And Thou didst beat back my weak gaze, pouring out Thy light upon me in its intensity; and I trembled with love and with horror. For I found myself to be far away from Thee in a land that was unlike Thee; it was as though I heard Thy Voice from on high, saying: "I am the Food of grown men, grow, and thou shalt eat Me, but thou shalt not be changed into Me" (*Confessions*, VII. x. 2).

S. Augustine: And the faithful are well aware of that Spiritual Food Which you, too, will soon know and Which you are to receive from God's altar. It will be your food, nay, your daily food, needful for this life. For are we not about to receive the Eucharist wherein we come to Christ Himself, and begin to reign with Him for ever? The Eucharist is our daily Bread. But let us so receive it as to be thereby refreshed, not in body merely but in mind. For the power which we know to be therein is the power of Unity whereby we are brought into union with His Body and become His members. Let us be What we receive; for then It will be truly our daily bread.

Again, what I set before you is your daily bread; and what you hear read day by day in the church is your daily bread; and the hymns you hear and which you sing—they are your daily bread. For these things we need for our pilgrimage. But when we get There are we going to hear a book read? Nay, we are going to hear the Word Himself; we are going to see the Word Himself; we are going to eat Him, to drink Him, even as the Angels do already. Do the Angels need books, or disputations, or readers? Nay, not so. But by seeing they read, for they see the Truth Itself and are sated from that Fount whence we receive but the sprinkling of the dew (*Sermon*, lvii., *on S. Matt.* vi. 7).

S. Augustine: When ye say *Give us this day our daily bread*, ye profess yourselves God's beggars. Yet blush not at it! The richest man on earth is God's beggar. The beggar stands at the rich man's door. But the rich man in his turn stands at the door of one richer than he. He is begged from, and he, too, has to beg. If he were not in need he would not beseech God in prayer. But what can the rich man need? I dare to say it: he needs even his daily bread! For how is it that he abounds with all things, save that God gave them to him? And what will they have if God but withdraw His hand? (*Sermon*, lvi. 9, *on S. Matt.* vi.).

S. Augustine: Think not that you have no need to say *Forgive us our trespasses as we forgive them that trespass against us*.... He who looks with pleasure at what he should not—sins. Yet who can control the glance of the eye? Indeed, some say that the eye is so called from its swiftness (*oculus a velocitate*). Who can control his eyes or his ears? You can close your eyes when you like, but how quickly they open again! You can shut your ears with an effort; put up your hand, and you can touch them. But if someone holds your hands your ears remain open, and you cannot then shut out cursing words, impure words, flattering and deceitful words. When you hear something which you should not—do you not sin with your ears? What when you hear some evil thing with pleasure? And the death-dealing tongue! How many sins it commits! (*Sermon*, lvi. 8).

S. Augustine: Indeed, our whole righteousness—true righteousness though it be, by reason of the True Good to Whom it is referred, consists rather, as long as we are in this life, in the remission of our sins than in the perfection of our virtues. And the proof of this is the Prayer of the whole City of God which is in pilgrimage on this earth. For by all Its members It cries to God: *Forgive us our trespasses as we forgive them the trespass against us!* And this Prayer is of no avail for those whose faith is without works—dead; but only for those whose faith worketh through charity. For though our reason is indeed subject to God, yet in this our mortal condition, in this corruptible body which weigheth down the soul, our reason does not perfectly control our vices, and hence such prayer as this is needful for the righteous (*Of the City of God*, xix. 27).

"Father, the hour is come; glorify Thy Son, that Thy Son may glorify Thee. As Thou hast given Him power over all flesh, that He may give life everlasting to all whom Thou hast given Him. And this is life everlasting, that they may know Thee, the only true God, and Jesus Christ, Whom Thou hast sent."

Rhythm in Honour of the Blessed Sacrament, said to have been composed by S. Thomas on his Death-Bed.

Adoro Te devote, latens Deitas,Quæ sub his figuris vere latitas;Tibi se cor meum totum subjicit,Quia Te contemplans totum deficit.

Visus, tactus gustus, in Te fallitur,Sed auditu solo tuto creditur;Credo quidquid dixit Dei Filius,Nil hoc verbo veritatis verius.

In cruce latebat sola Deitas,At hic latet simul et humanitas;Ambo tamen credens atque confitens,Peto quod petivit latro poenitens.

Plagas, sicut Thomas, non intueor,Deum tamen meum Te confiteor;Fac me Tibi semper magis credere,In Te spem habere, Te diligere.

O memoriale mortis Domini,Panis vivus, vitam præstans homini,Præsta meæ menti de Te vivero,Et Te illi semper dulce sapere.

Pie Pellicane Jesu Domine,Me immundum munda Tuo Sanguine,Cujus una stilla salvum facereTotum mundum quit ab omni scelere.

Jesu Quem velatum nunc aspicio,Oro fiat illud quod tam sitio,Ut Te revelata cernens facie,Visu sim beatus Tuæ gloriæ!

(An Indulgence of 100 days for the recitation of this rhythm. *S. Congr. of Indulgences,* December 20, 1884.)

X

Is Prayer Peculiar to Rational Creatures?

Prayer is an act of the reason, as we have shown above. And rational creatures are so termed because of the possession of reason. Consequently prayer is peculiar to them.

As we have said above, prayer is an act of the reason by which a person pleads with his superior, just in the same way as a command is an act of the reason by which an inferior is directed to do something. Prayer, then, properly pertains to one who has the use of reason and who also has a superior with whom he can plead. The Persons of the Trinity have no superior; the brute animals have no reason. Hence prayer belongs neither to the Divine Persons nor to the brute creation, but is peculiar to rational creatures.

Some, however, argue that prayer cannot be peculiar to rational creatures, thus:

1. To ask and to receive belong to the same person. But the Divine Persons receive: the Son, namely, and the Holy Spirit. Consequently They can also pray; indeed it is the Son Himself Who says, *I will ask the Father*, and the Apostle says of the Holy Spirit, *The Spirit Himself asketh for us.*

But it belongs to the Divine Persons to receive by Their nature, whereas to pray belongs to one who receives through grace. The Son is said to ask or pray according to the nature He took upon Himself—that is according to His Human, and not according to His Divine, Nature; the Holy Spirit, too, is said to petition because He makes us petition.

2. But further, the Angels are superior to the rational creation since they are intellectual substances; but it belongs to the Angels to pray, for it is said in the Psalm: *Adore Him, all ye His Angels.*

But the intellect and the reason are not different faculties in us, though they do differ in the sense that one is more perfect than the other. Consequently the intellectual creation, such as are the Angels, is sometimes distinguished from the rational creation, but at other times both are embraced under the one term "rational." And it is in this latter sense of the term "rational" that prayer is said to be peculiar to the rational creation.

3. Lastly, he prays who calls upon God; for it is chiefly by prayer that we call upon God. But the brute animals also call upon God, for the Psalmist says: *Who giveth to beasts their food, and to the young ravens that call upon Him.*

But the young ravens are said to call upon God by reason of those natural desires by which all things, each in their own fashion, desire to obtain the Divine goodness. In the same way brute animals are said to obey God by reason of the natural instinct by which they are moved by God.

"Reward them that patiently wait for Thee, that Thy Prophets may be found faithful: and hear the prayers of Thy servants. According to the blessing of Aaron over Thy people, and direct us into the way of justice, and let all know that dwell upon the earth, that Thou art God the beholder of all ages."

XI

Do the Saints in Heaven Pray for Us?

This is he who prayeth much for the people and for all the holy city, Jeremias the Prophet of God.

As S. Jerome says, Vigilantius's error lay in maintaining that "while we live we can mutually pray for one another; but after we are dead no one's prayer for another is heard, and this is especially clear in the case of the Martyrs who were unable to obtain by their prayers vengeance for their blood."

But this is altogether false; for since prayer for others springs from charity, the more perfect the charity of those who are in Heaven the more they pray for those wayfarers on earth who can be helped by their prayers. And the more knit they are to God the more efficacious are their prayers; for the Divine harmony demands that the superabundance of those who are in the higher position should redound upon those who are lower, just as the brightness of the sun renders the atmosphere itself luminous. Whence Christ Himself is said to be*Approaching of Himself to God to intercede for us.* Whence, too, S. Jerome's reply to Vigilantius: "If the Apostles and Martyrs, when they were still in the body, and had still to be solicitous on their own account, prayed for others, how much more when they have won the crown, when they have gained the victory and the triumph?"

Yet some maintain that the Blessed in Heaven do not pray for us, thus:

1. A man's acts are more meritorious for himself than for another. But the Saints who are in Heaven neither merit for themselves nor pray for themselves, for they have already attained the goal of their desires. Hence neither do they pray for us.

But the Saints who are in our Fatherland lack no Blessedness—since they are Blessed—save the glory of the body, and for this they pray. But they pray for us who still lack the ultimate perfection of Blessedness; and their prayers are efficacious by reason of their previous merits and of the Divine acceptation of their prayers.

2. But once more: the Saints are perfectly conformed to the Will of God, and consequently will nothing but what He wills. But what God wills is always fulfilled. Hence it is idle for the Saints to pray for us.

But the Saints obtain that which God wills should come about through the medium of their prayers; and they ask for what they think is, by God's Will, to be fulfilled through their prayers.

3. And yet again: just as the Saints in Heaven are superior to us so also are they who are in Purgatory—for they cannot sin. Those, however, who are in Purgatory do not pray for us, but rather we for them. It follows, then, that neither can the Saints in Heaven pray for us.

But though those who are in Purgatory are superior to us in that they cannot sin, yet are they our inferiors as regards the penalties they suffer; hence they are not in a state to pray for us, but rather we for them.

4. Once more: if the Saints in Heaven could pray for us it would follow that the prayers of the holiest Saints would be the most efficacious, and that consequently we ought not to ask the inferior Saints to pray for us, but only the greatest ones.

But God desires inferior things to be helped by all that are superior, and consequently we have to implore the aid of not only the chief Saints but also of the lesser; else it would follow that we ought to implore mercy from God alone. And it may sometimes happen that the petition made to a lesser Saint is more efficacious, either because we ask him more devoutly, or because God wishes thus to show forth his sanctity.

5. Lastly, Peter's soul is not Peter. Consequently if the souls of the Saints could pray for us, we ought—as long as their souls are separated from their bodies—to appeal, not to Peter to help us, but to Peter's soul; whereas the Church does the contrary. From which it would seem that the Saints, at all events previous to the Resurrection, do not pray for us.

But since the Saints merited when alive that they should pray for us, we therefore call upon them by the names they bore when here below, and by which they are best known to us; and we do this, too, in order to show our faith in the Resurrection, in accordance with the words *I am the God of Abraham.*

Cajetan: The question arises: how could Jeremias, who in the days of the Maccabees was not yet in our Fatherland but still in the Limbo of the Fathers, pray for Jerusalem?

But if we carefully consider what it is at root which makes the prayers of the Saints in the Fatherland avail for us, we shall find that the same reason holds for the Saints who were in Limbo as for those who enjoy the Beatific Vision. For it is their charity in their state of absolute superiority to us which is the reason for their praying for us. Hence, in the reply to the third difficulty, those who are in Purgatory are excluded from the number of those who pray for us because they are not altogether our superiors, but by reason of their sufferings are inferior to us, and need our prayers.

But the Fathers in Limbo were, it is clear, confirmed in charity and were incapable of sin, neither were they liable to any peculiar or fresh suffering. For while the pain of loss was common to them and to the sojourners on earth, the former were free from all pain of sense, hence they could pray for us. There is, however, this difference to be noted between them and the Saints in the Fatherland—viz., that whereas the former had it in common with the latter to pray for those sojourning on earth, it is given only to the Saints in the Fatherland to see the prayers of us sojourners addressed to them. Hence Jeremias is here said to pray, he is not said to have heard their prayers or supplications (*on* 2. 2. 83. 11).

XII

Should Prayer be Vocal?

I cried to the Lord with my voice, with my voice I made supplication to the Lord.

Prayer is of two kinds: public and private. *Public* or common prayer is that which is offered to God by the Church's ministers in the person of the whole body of the faithful. And it is necessary that such prayer should be known to the body of the faithful for whom it is offered; this, however, could not be unless it were vocal; consequently it is reasonably enacted that the Church's ministers should pronounce such prayers in a loud voice so as to reach the ears of all.

Private prayer, on the contrary, is that which is offered by private individuals, whether for themselves or for others; and its nature does not demand that it should be vocal. At the same time, we can use our voices in this kind of prayer, and this for three reasons: Firstly, in order to excite interior devotion whereby our minds may, when we pray, be lifted up to God; for men's minds are moved by external signs—whether words or acts—to understand, and, by consequence, also to feel. Wherefore S. Augustine says to Proba: "By words and other signs we vehemently stir ourselves up so as to increase our holy desires." Hence in private prayer we must make such use of words and other signs as shall avail to rouse our minds interiorly. But if, on the other hand, such things only serve to distract the mind, or prove in any way a hindrance, then we must cease from them; this is especially the case with those whose minds are sufficiently prepared for devotion without such incentives. Thus the Psalmist says: *My heart hath said to Thee, My face hath sought Thee;* and of Anna we are told that *she spoke within her heart.*

And secondly, we make use of vocal prayer in payment, as it were, of a just debt—in order, that is, to serve God with the entirety of what we have received from Him; consequently not with our mind alone but with our body as well; and this, as the Prophet Osee says, is especially suitable to prayer considered as a satisfaction for our sins: *Take away all iniquity and receive the good, and we will render the calves of our lips.*

And thirdly, we sometimes make use of vocal prayer because the soul overflows, as it were, on to the body by reason of the vehemence of our feelings, as it is written: *My heart hath been glad, and my tongue hath rejoiced.*

But it seems to some that prayer should not be vocal, thus:

1. Prayer is, as we have said, principally directed to God, and God knows the heart's speech. Consequently to add vocal prayer is idle.

45

But vocal prayer is not employed in order to manifest to God something which He did not know, but to stir up the mind of him who prays, and of others, too, towards God.

2. Again, man's mind is meant to rise by prayer towards God; but words, and other things pertaining to the senses, keep back a man from the ascent of contemplation.

Words appertaining to other things than God do indeed distract the mind and hinder the devotion of him who prays; but devotional words stir up the mind, especially if it be less devout.

3. Lastly, prayer ought to be offered to God in secret, according to the words: *But thou when thou shalt pray, enter into thy chamber, and having shut the door, pray to thy Father in secret;* whereas to pray vocally means to publish it abroad.

But, as S. Chrysostom says: "The Lord forbade us to pray in public with a view to being seen by the public. Consequently, when we pray we should do nothing novel to attract men's attention, whether by uttering cries which may be heard by them, or by openly beating our breasts, or by spreading out our hands, for the crowd to see us." While, on the other hand, as S. Augustine remarks: "To be seen by men is not wrong, but to do things to be seen by men."

Cajetan: Note carefully, ye who murmur at the Church's services, these three points: the different kinds of vocal prayer, its necessity, and the conditions attaching to it. For vocal prayer is divided into that which is in common and that which is private or individual.

The general necessity of vocal prayer arises from the fact that it is offered in the person of the Church. For since the Church is composed of created beings dependent on the senses, prayer made through the medium of the senses—*i.e.,* vocal prayer—must needs be offered by its ministers; else we should not know whether the worship of prayer was being offered by God's ministers, nor should we be conscious of the gift to God which was being offered by them in prayer; for the Church only judges from the things that appear externally.

Our individual need of vocal prayer arises from the necessity of stirring up our own devotion, and preserving it.

The conditions of prayer in common are twofold: it must be vocal, and it must be out loud. Hence those who say private Masses in such a low tone—and that consciously—as to be unintelligible to their hearers, appear to act unreasonably and are inexcusable, unless it should happen by accident that no one is present; in this case it is sufficient if they can be heard by the server who is close at hand. This will also show us what use we are to make of chant, or of recitation without chant, in prayer in common: it must be governed by our common devotion. And in whatever fashion such prayer may be made this rule must always be observed: it must be said so intelligibly that the meaning of the words may be distinctly perceived both by the reciters and by others, that so the Church's devotion may be aroused.

And reason tells us what conditions attach to our private prayer: viz., our own private devotion. This shews, too, the error of those who, in order to complete the tale of a large number of private vocal prayers each day, lay aside meditation and mental prayer. They neglect the end for the means (*on* 2. 2. 83. 12).

S. Augustine: Oh! How I lifted up my voice to Thee, O Lord, when I sang the Psalms of David, those songs full of faith, those strains full of piety which soothed my swelling spirit! And I was then but uninstructed in Thy true love; a catechumen spending my leisure with Alypius, another catechumen. And my mother stayed with us: clad indeed in woman's garb, but with a man's faith, with a matron's calm, with a mother's love, with a Christian's piety. Oh! How I lifted up my voice in those Psalms! How they inflamed my heart! How I yearned to recite them, if I could, to the whole world—as an answer to the pride of the human race! Though, indeed, they are sung throughout the world, and none can hide himself from Thy heat! (*Confess.*, IX. iv. 8).

S. Augustine: Sometimes, indeed, through immoderate fear of this mistake I err by excessive severity; nay, sometimes, though it is but rarely, I could almost wish to shut out from my ears and even from the Church itself all those sweet-sounding melodies used in the accompaniment of David's Psalms. Sometimes it seems to me as though it would be safer to do as I have often heard that Athanasius, the Bishop of Alexandria, did, for he made the reader of the Psalms so modulate his voice that he came to be rather speaking than singing. Yet, on the other hand, when I remember the tears which I shed when I heard the Church's chant in the early days of my regaining the faith, and when I notice that even now I am stirred—not so much by the chant as by the things that are chanted—when, that is, they are chanted with clear intonation and suitable modulation, then once more I recognize the great value of this appointed fashion (*Confess.*, X. xxxiii. 50).

S. Augustine: I have cried with my whole heart, hear me, O Lord! Who can question but that when men pray their cry to the Lord is vain if it be nought but the sound of the corporeal voice and their heart be not intent upon God? But if their prayer come from the heart, then, even though the voice of the body be silent, it may be hidden from all men, yet not from God. Whether, then, we pray to God with our voice—at times when such prayer is necessary—or whether we pray in silence, it is our heart that must send forth the cry. But the heart's cry is the earnest application of our minds. And when this accompanies our prayer it expresses the deep affections of him who yearns and asks and so despairs not of his request. And further, a man cries *with his whole heart* when he has no other thought. Such prayers with many are rare; with few are they frequent; I know not whether anyone's prayers are always so (*Enarr. in Ps.* cxviii., *Sermon*, xxix. I).

"Incline Thy ear, O Lord, and hear me; for I am needy and poor. Preserve my soul, for I am holy: save Thy servant, O my God, that trusteth in Thee. Have mercy on me, O Lord, for I have cried to Thee all the day. Give joy to the soul of Thy servant, for to Thee, O Lord, I have lifted up my soul. For Thou, O Lord, art sweet and mild; and plenteous in mercy to all that call upon Thee."

XIII

Must Prayer necessarily be Attentive?

That even holy men sometimes suffer distraction of mind when at prayer is clear from the words: *My heart hath forsaken me!*

This question particularly concerns vocal prayer. And for its solution we must know that a thing is said to be necessary in two senses: firstly, in the sense that by it a certain end is *more readily* attained, and in this sense attention is absolutely requisite in prayer. But a thing is said to be necessary also because without it a certain thing cannot attain its object *at all*. Now the effect or object of prayer is threefold. Its first effect—an effect, indeed, which is common to all acts springing from charity—is *merit*; but to secure this effect it is not necessarily required that attention should be kept up throughout the prayer, but the initial intention with which a man comes to prayer renders the whole prayer meritorious, as, indeed, is the case in all other meritorious acts.

The second effect of prayer is peculiar to it, and that is to *obtain favours*; and for this, too, the primary intention suffices, and to it God principally looks. But if the primary intention is wanting, prayer is not meritorious, neither can it win favours; for, as S. Gregory says, God hears not the prayer of a man who when he prays does not give heed to God.

The third effect of prayer is that which it immediately and actually brings about, namely, the *spiritual refreshment of the soul*; and to attain this end attention is necessarily required in prayer. Whence it is said, *If I pray in a tongue my understanding is without fruit.*

At the same time, we must remember that there is a threefold species of attention which may find place in our vocal prayer: one by which a man attends to the words he recites, and is careful to make no mistake in them; another by which he attends to the meaning of the words; and a third by which he attends to the end of all prayer—namely, God Himself—and to the object for which he is praying. And this species of attention is the most necessary of all, and one which even uninstructed folk can have; sometimes, indeed, the intensity with which the mind is borne towards God is, as says Hugh of S. Victor, so overwhelming that the mind is oblivious of all else.

Some, however, argue that prayer must of necessity be attentive, thus:

1. It is said in S. John's Gospel: *God is a spirit, and they that adore Him must adore Him in spirit and truth.* But inattentive prayer is not *in spirit.*

But he prays *in spirit and in truth* who comes to pray moved by the impulse of the Spirit, even though, owing to human infirmity, his mind afterwards wanders.

2. But again, prayer is "the ascent of the mind towards God." But when prayer is inattentive the mind does not ascend towards God.

But the human mind cannot, owing to Nature's weakness, long remain on high, for the soul is dragged down to lower things by the weight of human infirmity; and hence it happens that when the mind of one who prays ascends towards God in contemplation it suddenly wanders away from Him owing to his infirmity.

3. Lastly, prayer must needs be without sin. But not without sin does a man suffer distraction of mind when he prays, for he seems to mock God, just as if one were to speak with his fellow-man and not attend to what he said. Consequently S. Basil says: "The Divine assistance is to be implored, not remissly, nor with a mind that wanders here and there; for such a one not only will not obtain what he asks, but will rather be mocking God."

Of course, if a man purposely allowed his mind to wander in prayer, he would commit a sin and hinder the fruit of his prayer. Against such S. Augustine says in his *Rule*: "When you pray to God in Psalms and hymns, entertain your heart with what your lips are reciting." But that distraction of mind which is unintentional does not destroy the fruit of prayer.

Hence S. Basil also says: "But if through the weakness of sinful nature you cannot pray with attention, restrain your imagination as far as you can, and God will pardon you, inasmuch as it is not from negligence but from weakness that you are unable to occupy yourself with Him as you should."

Cajetan: Does a man satisfy the precept of the Church if, being bound to the recitation of the Divine Office, he sets out with the intention of meditating upon the Divine Goodness or upon the Passion of Christ, and thus keeping his mind firmly fixed upon God? Clearly a man who strives to keep his mind occupied during the whole of the Divine Office with contemplation of and devout affections towards God and Divine things fully satisfies his obligation. So, too, a man who aims at meditation on the Passion of Christ and devout affections on it during the whole Office, undoubtedly satisfies his obligation, for he is making use of a better means for keeping in touch with the Divinity than if he merely dwelt upon the meaning of the words. At the same time, he must be ready to lay this aside if in the course of the Office he finds himself uplifted to Divine things, for at this he must primarily aim. One who so prays, then, must make the Passion of Christ a means and not an end; he must, that is, be prepared to ascend thereby, if God grants it, to Divine things. In short, we may make use of any one of the species of attention enumerated above provided we do not exclude the higher forms. Thus, for example, if a man feels that it is more suited to his small capacity to aim simply at making no mistakes, and habitually makes use of this form of attention, he must still use it as a means only; he must, that is, be at God's disposition, for God may have mercy upon him and grant him, by reason of his dispositions, some better form of attention.

Again, when a person prays for things needful for his support in life he must not be so occupied with the thought of these things as to appear to subordinate Divine things to human, as though prayer was but a means and his daily living the end. We must bear in mind the doctrine laid down above—viz., that *all our prayers should tend to the attainment of grace and glory*. We must occupy ourselves with the thought of eternal glory, or of the glory of the adoption of sons during this life, or with the virtues as means to arriving at our eternal home, and as the adornment of the inhabitants of heaven, and the commencement here of heavenly "conversation"; such things as these must be counted as the highest forms of attention (*on* 2. 2. 83. 13).

S. Augustine: *Give joy to the soul of Thy servant, for to Thee, O Lord, I have lifted up my soul. For Thou, O Lord, art sweet and mild.* It seems to me that he calls God "mild" because He endures all our vagaries, and only awaits our prayers that He may perfect us. And when we offer Him our prayers He accepts them gratefully and hears them. Neither does He reflect on the careless way in which we pour them out, He even accepts prayers of which we are hardly conscious! For, Brethren, what man is there who would put up with it if a friend of his began a conversation with him, and yet, just when he was ready to reply to what his friend said, should discover that he was paying no attention to him but was saying something to someone else? Or supposing you were to appeal to a judge and were to appoint a place for him to hear your appeal, and then suddenly, while you were talking with him, were to put him aside and begin to gossip with a friend! How long would he put up with you? And yet God puts up with the hearts of so many who pray to Him and who yet are thinking of other things, even evil things, even wicked things, things hateful to God; for even to think of unnecessary things is an insult to Him with Whom you have begun to talk. For your prayer is a conversation with God. When you read, God speaks to you; when you pray, you speak to God.... And you may picture God saying to you: "You forget how often you have stood before Me and have thought of such idle and superfluous things and have so rarely poured out to Me an attentive and definite prayer!" But *Thou, O Lord, art sweet and mild!* Thou art sweet, bearing with me! It is from weakness that I slip away! Heal me and I shall stand; strengthen me and I shall be firm! But until Thou dost so, bear with me, for *Thou, O Lord, art sweet and mild* (*Enarr. in Ps.* lxxxv. 7).

S. Augustine: *Praise the Lord, O my soul!* What mean these words, Brethren? Do we not praise the Lord? Do we not sing hymns day by day? Do not our mouths, each according to their measure, sound forth day by day the praises of God? And what is it we praise? It is a great Thing that we praise, but that wherewith we praise is weak as yet. When does the singer fill up the praises of Him Whom he sings? A man stands and sings before God, often for a long space; but oftentimes, whilst his lips move to frame the words of his song, his thoughts fly away to I know not what desires! And so, too, our mind has sometimes been fixed on praising God in a definite manner, but our soul has flitted away, led hither and thither by divers desires and anxious cares. And then our mind, as though from up above, has looked down upon the soul as it flitted to and fro, and has seemed to turn to it and address its uneasy wanderings—saying to it: *Praise the Lord, O my soul!* Why art thou anxious about other things than Him? Why busy thyself with the mortal things of earth? And then our soul, as though weighed down and unable to stand firm as it should, replies to our mind: *I will praise the Lord in my life!* Why does it say *in my life*? Why? Because now I am in my death!

Rouse yourself, then, and say: *Praise the Lord, O my soul!* And your soul will reply to you: "I praise Him as much as I can, though it is but weakly, in small measure, and with little strength." But why so? Because *while we are in the body we are absent from the Lord.* And why do you thus praise the Lord so imperfectly and with so little fixity of attention? Ask Holy Scripture: *The corruptible body weigheth down the soul, and the earthly habitation presseth down the mind that museth upon many things.* O take away, then, my body which weigheth down the soul, and then will I praise the Lord! Take away my earthly habitation which presseth down the mind that museth upon many things, so that, instead of many things I may be occupied with One Thing alone, and may praise the Lord! But as long as I am as I am, I cannot, for I am weighed down! What then? Wilt thou be silent? Wilt thou never perfectly praise the Lord? *I will praise the Lord in my life!* (*Enarr in Ps.* cxlv. I).

"My spirit is in anguish within me; my heart within me is troubled. I remembered the days of old, I meditated on all Thy works; I meditated upon the works of Thy hands. I stretched forth my hands to Thee; my soul is as earth without water unto Thee. Hear me speedily, O Lord: my spirit hath fainted away."

S. Thomas: The fruits of prayer are twofold. For first there is the merit which thereby accrues to a man; and, secondly, there is the spiritual consolation and devotion which is begotten of prayer. And he who does not attend to, or does not understand his prayer, loses that fruit which is spiritual consolation; but we cannot say that he loses that fruit which is merit, for then we should have to say that very many prayers were without merit since a man can hardly say the *Lord's Prayer* without some distraction of mind. Hence we must rather say that when a person is praying and is sometimes distracted from what he is saying, or—more generally—when a person is occupied with some meritorious work and does not continuously and at every moment reflect that he is doing it for God, his work does not cease to be meritorious. And the reason is that in meritorious acts directed to a right end it is not requisite that our intention should be referred to that end at every moment, but the influence of the intention with which we begun persists throughout even though we now and again be distracted in some particular point; and the influence of this initial intention renders the whole body of what we do meritorious unless it be broken off by reason of some contrary affection intruding itself and diverting us from the end we had first in view to some other end contrary to it.

And it must be remembered that there are three kinds of attention. The first is attention to the words we are actually saying; and sometimes this is harmful, for it may hinder devotion. The second is attention to the meaning of the words, and this, too, may be harmful, though not gravely so. The third is attention to the goal of our prayer, and this better and almost necessary (*Commentary on I Cor.* xiv. 14).

XIV

Should our Prayers be Long?

It would seem that we ought to pray continuously, for our Lord said: *We ought always to pray and not to faint;* so also S. Paul: *Pray without ceasing.*

But we must notice that when we speak of prayer we can mean either prayer *considered in itself* or the *cause of prayer.* Now the *cause of prayer* is the desire of the love of God; and all prayer ought to spring from this desire which is, indeed, continuous in us, whether actually or virtually, since this desire virtually remains in everything which we do from charity. But we ought to do all things for the glory of God: *whether you eat or whether you drink, or whatsoever else you do, do all to the glory of God.* In this sense, then, prayer ought to be continual. Hence S. Augustine says to Proba: "Therefore by our faith, by our hope, and by our charity, we are always praying, for our desire is continued."

But *prayer considered in itself* cannot be so continuous; for we must needs be occupied with other things. Hence S. Augustine says in the same place: "At certain intervals, at divers hours and times, we pray to God in words so that by these outward signs of things we may admonish ourselves, and may learn what progress we have made in this same desire, and may stir ourselves up to increase it."

But the quantity of a thing has to be determined by its purpose, just as a draught has to be proportioned to the health of the man who takes it. Consequently it is fitting that prayer should only last so long as it avails to stir up in us this fervour of interior desire. And when it exceeds this measure, and its prolongation only results in weariness, it must not be prolonged further. Hence S. Augustine also says to Proba: "The Brethren in Egypt are said to have had frequent prayers; but they were exceedingly brief, hardly more than eager ejaculations; and they adopted this method lest, if they prolonged their prayer, that vigilant attention which is requisite for prayer should lose its keen edge and become dulled. And thus they clearly show that this same attention, just as it is not to be forced if it fails to last, so neither is it to be quickly broken off if it does last."

And just as we have to pay attention to this in our private prayers, and have to be guided by our powers of attention, so must we observe the same principles in public prayer where we have to be governed by the people's devotion.

Some, however, argue that our prayers ought not to be continual, thus:

1. Our Lord said: *And when you are praying speak not much.* But it is not easy to see how a man can pray long without "speaking much"; more especially if it is a question of vocal prayer.

But S. Augustine says to Proba: "To prolong our prayer does not involve 'much-speaking.' 'Much-speaking' is one thing; the unceasing desire of the heart is another. Indeed we are told

52

of the Lord Himself that *He passed the whole night in the prayer of God*; and, again, that *being in an agony He prayed the longer*, and this that He might afford us an example." And Augustine adds a little later: "Much speaking in prayer is to be avoided, but not much petition, if fervent attention lasts. For 'much-speaking' in prayer means the use of superfluous words when we pray for something necessary; but much petition means that with unceasing and devout stirrings of the heart we knock at His door to Whom we pray; and this is often a matter rather of groans than of words, of weeping than of speaking."

2. Further, prayer is but the unfolding of our desires. But our desires are holy in proportion as they are confined to one thing, in accordance with those words of the Psalmist: *One thing I have asked of the Lord, this will I seek after.* Whence it would seem to follow that our prayers are acceptable to God just in proportion to their brevity. But to prolong our prayer does not mean that we ask for many things, but that our hearts are continuously set upon one object for which we yearn.

3. Once more, it is unlawful for a man to transgress the limits which God Himself has fixed, especially in matters which touch the Divine worship, according to the words: *Charge the people lest they should have a mind to pass the limits to see the Lord, and a very great multitude of them should perish.* But God Himself has assigned limits to our prayer by instituting the *Lord's Prayer*, as is evident from the words: *Thus shalt thou pray.* Hence we ought not to extend our prayer beyond these limits. But our Lord did not institute this prayer with a view to tying us down exclusively to these words when we pray, but to show us that the scope of our prayer should be limited to asking only for the things contained in it, whatever form of words we may use or whatever may be our thoughts.

4. And lastly, with regard to the words of our Lord *that we ought always to pray and not to faint*, and those of S. Paul, *Pray without ceasing*, we must remark that a man prays without ceasing, either because of the unceasing nature of his desire, as we have above explained; or because he does not fail to pray at the appointed times; or because of the effect which his prayer has, whether upon himself—since even when he has finished praying he still remains devout—or upon others, as, for instance, when a man by some kind action induces another to pray for him whereas he himself desists from his prayer.

"Our soul waiteth for the Lord; for He is our helper and protector. For in Him our hearts shall rejoice; and in His Holy Name we have trusted. Let Thy mercy, O Lord, be upon us, as we have hoped in Thee."

XV

Is Prayer Meritorious?

On the words of the Psalmist, *My prayer shall be turned into my bosom*, the interlinear Gloss has: "And if it is of no profit to them (for whom it is offered), at least I myself shall not lose my reward." A reward, however, can only be due to merit. Prayer, then, is meritorious.

As we have said above, prayer has, besides the effect of spiritual consolation which it brings with it, a twofold power regarding the future: the power, namely, of meriting, and that of winning favours. But prayer, as indeed every other virtuous act, derives its power of meriting from that root which is charity, and the true and proper object of charity is that Eternal Good, the enjoyment of Which we merit. Now prayer proceeds from charity by means of the virtue of religion whose proper act is prayer; there accompany it, however, certain other virtues which are requisite for a good prayer—namely, faith and humility. For it belongs to the virtue of religion to offer our prayers to God; while to charity belongs the desire of that the attainment of which we seek in prayer. And faith is necessary as regards God to Whom we pray; for we must, of course, believe that from Him we can obtain what we ask. Humility, too, is called for on the part of the petitioner, for he must acknowledge his own needs. And devotion also is necessary; though this comes under religion of which it is the first act, it conditions all subsequent effects.

And its power of obtaining favours prayer owes to the grace of God to Whom we pray, and Who, indeed, induces us to pray. Hence S. Augustine says: "He would not urge us to ask unless He were ready to give"; and S. Chrysostom says: "He never refuses His mercies to them who pray, since it is He Who in His loving-kindness stirs them up so that they weary not in prayer."

But some say that prayer cannot be meritorious, thus:

1. Merit proceeds from grace, but prayer precedes grace, since it is precisely by prayer that we win grace: *Your Father from Heaven will give the Good Spirit to them that ask Him.*

But prayer, like any other virtuous act, cannot be meritorious without that grace which makes us pleasing to God. Yet even that prayer which wins for us the grace which renders us pleasing to God must proceed from some grace—that is, from some gratuitous gift; for, as S. Augustine says, to pray at all is a gift of God.

2. Again, prayer cannot be meritorious, for if it were so it would seem natural that prayer should especially merit that for which we actually pray. Yet this is not always the case, for even the prayers of the Saints are often not heard; S. Paul, for example, was not heard when he prayed that the sting of the flesh might be taken away from him.

But we must notice that the merit of our prayers sometimes lies in something quite different from what we beg for. For whereas merit is to be especially referred to the possession of God, our petitions in our prayers at times refer directly to other things, as we have pointed out above. Consequently, if what a man asks for will not tend to his ultimate attainment of God, he does not merit it by his prayer; sometimes, indeed, by asking and desiring such a thing he may lose all merit, as, for example, if a man were to ask of God something which was sinful and which he could not reverently ask for. Sometimes, however, what he asks for is not necessary for his salvation, nor yet is it clearly opposed to his salvation; and when a man so prays he may by his prayer merit eternal life, but he does not merit to obtain what he actually asks for. Hence S. Augustine says: "He who asks of God in faith things needful for this life is sometimes mercifully heard and sometimes mercifully not heard. For the physician knows better than the patient what will avail for the sick man." It was for this reason that Paul was not heard when he asked that the sting of the flesh might be taken away—it was not expedient. But if what a man asks for will help him to the attainment of God, as being something conducive to his salvation, he will merit it, and that not only by praying for it but also by doing other good works; hence, too, he undoubtedly will obtain what he asks for, but when it is fitting that he should obtain it: "for some things are not refused to us but are deferred, to be given at a fitting time," as S. Augustine says. Yet even here hindrance may arise if a man does not persevere in asking; hence S. Basil says: "When then you ask and do not receive, this is either because you asked for what you ought not, or because you asked without lively faith, or carelessly, or for what would not profit you, or because you ceased to ask." And since a man cannot, absolutely speaking, merit eternal life for another, nor, in consequence, those things which belong to eternal life, it follows that a man is not always heard when he prays for another. For a man, then, always to obtain what he asks, four conditions must concur: he must ask for himself, for things necessary for salvation; he must ask piously and perseveringly.

3. Lastly, prayer essentially reposes upon faith, as S. James says: *But let him ask in faith, nothing wavering.* But faith is not sufficient for merit, as is evident in the case of those who have faith without charity. Therefore prayer is not meritorious.

But while it is true that prayer rests principally upon faith, this is not for its power of meriting—for as regards this it rests principally on charity—but for its power of winning favours; for through faith man knows of the Divine Omnipotence and Mercy whence prayer obtains what it asks.

S. Augustine: Men, then, love different things, and when each one seemeth to have what he loves, he is called happy. But a man is truly happy, not if he has what he loves, but if he loves what ought to be loved. For many become more wretched through having what they love than they were when they lacked it. Miserable enough through loving harmful things, more miserable through having them. And our Merciful God, when we love amiss, denies us what we love; but sometimes in His anger He grants a man what he loves amiss!... But when we love what God wishes us to love, then, doubtless, He will give it us. This is That One Thing Which ought to be loved: that we may dwell in the House of the Lord all the days of our life! (*Enarr. in Ps.* xxvi.).

S. Augustine: In those tribulations, then, which can both profit us and harm us, we know not what we should pray for as we ought. Yet none the less since they are hard, since they are vexatious, since, too, they are opposed to our sense of our own weakness, mankind with one consent prays that they may be removed from us. But we owe this much devotion to the Lord our God that, if He refuses to remove them, we should not therefore fancy that we are neglected by Him, but, while bearing these woes with devout patience, we should hope for some greater good, for thus is power perfected in infirmity. Yet to some in their impatience the Lord God grants in anger what they ask, just as in His mercy He refused it to the Apostle (*Ep.* cxxx. *ad Probam*).

"Hear my prayer, O Lord, and my supplication; give ear to my tears. Be not silent: for I am a stranger with Thee, and a sojourner as all my fathers were. O forgive me, that I may be refreshed; before I go hence, and be no more."

XVI

Do Sinners gain Anything From God by their Prayers?

S. Augustine says: "If God did not hear sinners, in vain would the publican have said, *God be merciful to me a sinner*"; and S. Chrysostom says: "*Every one that asketh receiveth*—that is, whether he be just man or sinner." Hence the prayers of sinners do win something from God.

In a sinner we have to consider two things: his nature, which God loves; his fault, which God hates. If, then, a sinner asks something of God formally as a sinner—that is, according to his sinful desires—God, out of His mercy, does not hear him, though sometimes He does hear him in His vengeance, as when He permits a sinner to fall still farther into sin. For God "in mercy refuses some things which in anger He concedes," as S. Augustine says. But that prayer of a sinner which proceeds from the good desire of his nature God hears, not, indeed, as bound in justice to do so, for that the sinner cannot merit, but out of His pure mercy, and on condition, too, that the four above-mentioned conditions are observed—namely, that he prays for himself, for things needful for his salvation, that he prays devoutly and perseveringly.

Some, however, maintain that sinners do not by their prayers win anything from God, thus:

1. It is said in the Gospel, *Now we know that God doth not hear sinners*, and this accords with those words of *Proverbs; He that turneth away his ears from hearing the law, his prayer shall be an abomination.* But a prayer which is "an abomination" cannot win anything from God.

But, as S. Augustine remarks, the words first quoted are due to the blind man as yet unanointed—viz., not yet perfectly illumined—and hence they are not valid; though they might be true if understood of a sinner precisely as such, and in this sense, too, his prayer is said to be "an abomination."

2. Again, just men obtain from God what they merit, as we have said above. Sinners, however, can merit nothing, since they are without grace, and even without charity which, according to the Gloss on the words, *Having an appearance of piety, but denying the power thereof,* is "the *power* of piety." And hence they cannot pray piously, which, as we have said above, is requisite if prayer is to gain what it asks for.

But though a sinner cannot pray piously in the sense that his prayer springs from the habit of virtue, yet his prayer can be pious in the sense that he asks for something conducive to piety, just as a man who has not got the habit of justice can yet wish for some just thing, as we have pointed out above. And though such a man's prayer is not meritorious, it may yet have the power of winning favours; for while merit reposes upon justice, the power of winning favours reposes upon grace.

3. Lastly, S. Chrysostom says: "The Father does not readily hear prayers not dictated by the Son." But in the prayer which Christ dictated it is said: *Forgive us our debts as we also forgive our debtors*, which sinners do not. Hence sinners either lie when they say this prayer, and so do not deserve to be heard, or, if they do not say it, then they are not heard because they do not make use of the form of prayer instituted by Christ.

But, as we have explained above, the *Lord's Prayer* is spoken in the name of the whole Church. Consequently, if a man—while unwilling to forgive his neighbour his debts—yet says this prayer, he does not lie; for while what he says is not true as regards himself, it yet remains true as regards the Person of the Church outside of which he deservedly is, and he loses, in consequence, the fruit of his prayer. Sometimes, however, sinners are ready to forgive their debtors, and consequently their prayers are heard, in accordance with those words of Ecclesiasticus: *Forgive thy neighbour if he hath hurt thee, and then shall thy sins be forgiven to thee when thou prayest.*

"With the Lord shall the steps of a man be directed, and he shall like well his way. When he shall fall, he shall not be bruised, for the Lord putteth His hand under him. I have been young, and now am old; and I have not seen the just forsaken, nor his seed seeking bread."

XVII

Can We rightly term Supplications," "Prayers," "Intercessions," and "Thanksgivings," parts of Prayer?

The Apostle says to Timothy: *I desire therefore first of all that supplications, prayers, intercessions, and thanksgivings be made by all men.*

For prayer three things are required: first of all, that he who prays come nigh to God; and this is signified by the name *prayer*, for prayer is "the uplifting of the mind towards God." Secondly, petition is required, and is signified by the word *postulation*; now a petition may be set forth in definite terms—and this some term *postulation*, properly so called; or it may be set forth in no express terms, as when a man asks for God's help, and this some call *supplication*; or, again, the fact in question may be simply narrated, as in S. John: *He whom Thou lovest is sick*, and this some call *insinuation*. And thirdly, there is required a reason for asking for what we pray for, and this reason may be either on the part of God or on the part of the petitioner. The reason for asking on the part of God is His holiness, by reason of which we ask to be heard: *Incline Thine ear and hear ... for Thine own sake, O my God*; to this belongs *obsecration*—namely, an appeal to sacred things, as when we say: *By Thy Nativity, deliver us, O Lord!* But the reason for asking on the part of the petitioner is thankfulness, for by giving thanks for benefits already received we merit to receive still greater ones, as is set forth in the Church's *Collect.* Hence the Gloss says that in the Mass "*Obsecrations* are the prayers which precede the Consecration," for in them we commemorate certain sacred things; "in the Consecration itself we have *prayers*," for then the mind is especially uplifted towards God; "but in the subsequent petitions we have *postulations*, and at the close *thanksgivings*." These four parts of prayer may be noticed in many of the Church's *Collects*: thus in the *Collect* for Trinity Sunday, the words *Almighty and Everlasting God* signify the uplifting of the soul in prayer to God; the words: *Who hast granted to Thy servants to acknowledge in their profession of the true faith the glory of the Eternal Trinity, and in the Power of Its Majesty to adore Its Unity*, signify giving of thanks; the words: *Grant, we beseech Thee, that by perseverance in this same faith we may be ever defended from all adversities*, signify postulation; while the closing words: *Through our Lord Jesus Christ*, etc., signify obsecration.

In the *Conferences of the Fathers*, however, we read: "*Obsecration* is imploring pardon for sin; *prayer* is when we make vows to God; *postulation* is when we make petition for others; *giving of thanks*, those ineffable outpourings by which the mind renders thanks to God." But the former explanation is preferable.

Some, however, object to these divisions of prayer, thus:

I. *Obsecration* is apparently *to swear by someone*, whereas Origen remarks: "A man who desires to live in accordance with the Gospel must not swear by anyone, for if it is not allowed to swear, neither is it allowed to swear by anyone."

But it is sufficient to remark that *obsecration* is not a swearing by, or adjuring of God, as though to compel Him, for this is forbidden, but to implore His mercy.

2. Again, S. John Damascene says that prayer is "the asking God for things that are fitting." Hence it is not exact to distinguish *prayers* from *postulations*.

But prayer, generally considered, embraces all the above-mentioned parts; when, however, we distinguish one part against another, *prayer*, properly speaking, means the uplifting of the mind to God.

3. Lastly, giving of thanks refers to the past, whereas the other parts of prayer refer to the future. Hence giving of thanks should not be placed after the rest.

But whereas in things which are different from one another the past precedes the future, in one and the same thing the future precedes the past. Hence giving of thanks for benefits already received precedes petition; yet those same benefits were first asked for, and then, when they had been received, thanks were offered for them. Prayer, however, precedes petition, for by it we draw nigh to God to Whom we make petition. And *obsecration* precedes *prayer*, for it is from dwelling upon the Divine Goodness that we venture to approach to Him.

Cajetan: We might be asked how the mind can be especially elevated to God at the moment of consecration. For in the consecration the priest has to express distinctly the words of consecration, and consequently cannot have his mind uplifted towards God at that moment. Indeed, the more his mind is uplifted to God, the less he thinks of inferior things, words, and so forth.

But in the consecration of the Holy Eucharist—in which the priest in a sense brings God down upon earth—the very greatness of our uplifting of mind towards the Divine Goodness Which has thus deigned to come amongst us is the very reason for our attention to the words in the act of consecration, and makes the priest pronounce them distinctly and reverently. Some scrupulous folk, however, concentrate their whole attention on being intent and attentive; but this is really a distraction, and not attention, for its object is precisely the being attentive. The uplifting, then, of our minds to God in the consecration has indeed to be the very greatest, not, indeed, intensively and by abstraction from the things of sense, but objectively and concentrated—though always within the limits compatible with attention— on the endeavour to say the words as they should be said (*on* 2. 2. 83. 17.)

S. Augustine: And David went in and sat before the Lord; and Elias, casting himself down upon the earth, put his face between his knees. By examples such as these we are taught that there is no prescribed position of the body in prayer provided the soul states its intention in the presence of God. For we pray standing, as it is written: *The Publican standing afar off.* We pray, too, on our knees, as we read in the Acts of the Apostles; and we pray sitting, as in the case of David and Elias. And unless it were lawful to pray lying down, it would not be said in the Psalms: *Every night I will wash my bed, I will water my couch with my tears.* When, then, a man desires to pray, he settles himself in any position that serves at the time for the stirring up of his soul. When, on the other hand, we have no definite intention of praying, but the wish to pray suddenly occurs to us—when, that is, there comes of a sudden into our mind something which rouses the desire to pray "with unspeakable groanings"—then, in whatsoever position such a feeling may find us, we are not to put off our prayer; we are not to look about for some place whither we can withdraw, for some place in which to stand or in which to make prostration. For the very intention of the mind begets a solitude, and we often forget to which quarter of the heavens we were looking, or in what bodily position the occasion found us (*Of Divers Questions,* iv.).

"Hear, O God, my prayer, and despise not my supplication; be attentive to me and hear me. I am grieved in my exercise; and am troubled at the voice of the enemy, and at the tribulation of the sinner. For they have cast iniquities upon me, and in wrath they were troublesome to me. My heart is troubled within me, and the fear of death is fallen upon me. Fear and trembling are come upon me, and darkness hath covered me. And I said: Who will give me wings like a dove, and I will fly and be at rest?"

FROM THE SUPPLEMENT TO THE SUMMA—QUESTION LXXII

OF THE PRAYERS OF THE SAINTS WHO ARE IN HEAVEN

I

Are the Saints cognizant of our Prayers?

On those words of Job, *Whether his children come to honour or dishonour, he shall not understand*, S. Gregory says: "This is not to be understood of the souls of the Saints, for they see from within the glory of Almighty God, it is in nowise credible that there should be anything without of which they are ignorant."

And he says also: "To the soul that sees its Creator all created things are but trifling; for, however little of the Creator's light he sees, all that is created becomes of small import to him." Yet the greatest difficulty in saying that the souls of the Saints know our prayers and other things which concern us, is their distance from us. But since, according to the authority just quoted, this distance does not preclude such knowledge, it appears that the souls of the Saints do know our prayers and other things which concern us.

Further, if they did not know what concerned us, neither would they pray for us, since they would not know our deficiencies. But this was the error of Vigilantius, as S. Jerome says in his Epistle against him. The Saints, then, know what concerns us.

The Divine Essence, then, is a sufficient medium for knowing all things, as, indeed, is evident from the fact that God in seeing His own essence sees all things. Yet it does not follow that whoever sees the Essence of God therefore sees all things, but those only who *comprehend* the Essence of God; just in the same way as it does not follow that because we know a principle we therefore know all that that principle contains, for that would only be the case if we *comprehended* the whole power of the principle. Since, then, the souls of the Saints do not comprehend the Divine Essence, it does not follow that they know everything which could be known through the medium of that Divine Essence. Hence the inferior Angels are taught certain things by the higher Angels, though all see the Divine Essence. But each person in possession of the Beatific Vision only sees in the Divine Essence as much of other things as is necessitated by the degree of perfection of his beatitude; and for the perfection of beatitude it is required that a man "should have whatever he wants, and should desire nothing in an inordinate fashion." Each one, however, rightly desires to know those things which concern himself. Hence, since no rectitude is lacking to the Saints, they wish to know those things which concern themselves, and consequently they must know them in the Word. But it belongs to their glory that they should be able to help on the salvation of those who need it, for it is thus that they are made co-workers with God—"than which there is nought more Divine," as Denis says. It is clear, then, that the Saints have a knowledge of those things which are requisite for this end. And so, too, it is manifest that they know in the Word the desires, the devout acts and the prayers, of men who fly to them for help.

Some, however, maintain that the Saints do not know our prayers, thus:

1. On the words of Isaias, *Thou art our Father, and Abraham hath not known us, and Israel hath been ignorant of us*, the Interlinear Gloss has: "For the Saints who are dead know not what the living do, even their own children." This is taken from S. Augustine's treatise *On Care for the Dead*, xiii., where he quotes these words, and adds: "If these great Patriarchs were ignorant of what concerned those whom they had begotten, how can the dead be concerned with knowing and assisting the affairs and the deeds of the living?" Hence it would seem that the Saints are not cognizant of our prayers.

But these words of S. Augustine are to be understood of the natural knowledge of the souls separated (from this world); and this knowledge is not obscured in holy men as it is in sinners. Moreover, S. Augustine is not talking of that knowledge which is in the Word, a knowledge which it is clear that Abraham had not at the time that Isaias said these things; for anterior to Christ's Passion no one had attained to the Vision of God.

2. In 4 Kings xxii. 20, it is said to Josias the king: *Therefore*—because, that is, thou didst weep before Me—*I will gather thee to thy fathers ... that thy eyes may not see all the evils which I will bring upon this place*. But the death of Josias would have been no relief to him if he was to know after death what was going to happen to his nation. The Saints, then, who are dead, do not know our acts, and consequently cannot understand our prayers.

But although after this life the Saints know the things which are done here below, we are not therefore to suppose that they are filled with grief at the knowledge of the afflictions of those whom they loved in the world. For they are so filled with the joy of their beatitude that sorrow finds no place in them. Hence, if they know after death the evil plight of those dear to them, it is none the less a relief to their sorrow if they are withdrawn from this world before those woes come on.

At the same time it is possible that souls not yet in glory would feel a certain grief if they were made aware of the sorrows of those dear to them. And since the soul of Josias was not immediately glorified on its quitting the body, S. Augustine endeavours to argue that the souls of the dead have no knowledge of the deeds of the living.

3. Again, the more a person is perfected in charity the more ready he is to succour his neighbour in peril. But the Saints while still in the flesh had a care for their neighbours, and especially for their relatives, when in peril. Since, then, they are after death far more perfected in charity, if they were cognizant of our deeds, they would have now a much greater care for those dear to them or related to them, and would help them much more in their necessities; but this does not seem to be the case. Whence it would seem that they are not cognizant of our actions nor of our prayers.

But the souls of the Saints have their will perfectly conformed to the Will of God, even in what they would will. Consequently, while retaining their feelings of charity towards their neighbour, they afford them no other assistance than that which they see is arranged for them in accordance with Divine Justice. Yet at the same time we must believe that they help their neighbours very much indeed by interceding for them with God.

4. Further, just as the Saints after death see the Word, so also do the Angels, for of them it is said: *Their Angels in Heaven always see the face of My Father Who is in Heaven.* But the Angels, though seeing the Word, do not therefore know all things, for the inferior Angels are purified of their ignorance by the superior Angels, as is evident from Denis. Consequently, neither do the Saints, although they see the Word, know in It our prayers and other things which concern us.

But although it is not necessary that those who see the Word should see all things in the Word, they none the less see those things which belong to the perfection of their beatitude, as we have said above.

5. Lastly, God alone is the Searcher of hearts. But prayer is essentially an affair of the heart. Consequently God alone knows our prayers.

But God alone knows of Himself the thoughts of the heart; others know them according as they are revealed to them either in their vision of the Word or in any other way.

II

Ought we to appeal to the Saints to intercede for us?

In the Book of Job, it is said: *Call now, if there be any that will answer thee; and turn to some of the Saints.* And on this S. Gregory says: "It is our business to call, and to beseech God in humble prayer." When, then, we desire to pray to God, we ought to turn to the Saints that they may pray for us.

Further, the Saints who are in the Fatherland are more acceptable in the sight of God than they were when upon earth. But we ought to ask the Saints even when on earth to be our intercessors with God, as the Apostle shows us by his example when he says: *I beseech you, therefore, brethren, through our Lord Jesus Christ, and by the charity of the Holy Ghost, that you help me in your prayers for me to God.* Much more, then, should we ask the Saints who are in our Fatherland to help us by their prayers to God.

Moreover, the common custom of the Church confirms this, since in her Litanies she asks the prayers of the Saints.

In the words of Denis, "there is this Divinely established harmony in things—that they which hold the lowest place should be brought to God through them that come between them and God." Since, then, the Saints who are in our Fatherland are most nigh to God, the harmony of the Divine Government demands that we who, abiding in the body, are "absent from the Lord," should be led to Him by the Saints who stand midway; and this is secured when through their means the Divine Goodness pours out Its effects upon us. And since our return to God ought to correspond to the orderly way in which His goodnesses flow upon us—for His benefits flow out upon us through the intervention of the Saints' suffrages for us—so also ought we to be brought back to God through the intervention of the Saints, and thus once more receive His benefits. Whence it is that we make them our intercessors for us with God—and, as it were, mediators—by begging them to pray for us.

But some say that we should not ask the Saints to pray for us, thus:

1. No one asks a man's friends to intercede for him except in so far as he thinks that he can obtain a favour more easily through them. But God is infinitely more merciful than any Saint, and consequently His Will is more readily inclined to hear us than is the will of any Saint. Whence it would seem superfluous to make the Saints mediators between ourselves and God, and so ask them to intercede for us.

But just as it is not by reason of any deficiency on the part of the Divine Power that It works through the mediumship of secondary causes, whereas it rather tends to the fulfilment of the harmony of the universe that His Goodness should be more copiously diffused upon things, so that things not only receive from Him their own peculiar goodness, but themselves become a source of goodness to other things as well; so in the same way it is not by reason of any lack of mercy on His part that appeal to His mercy by means of the prayers of the Saints is fitting; but this is done in order that the aforesaid harmony may be preserved.

2. If we ought to ask the Saints to pray for us, it can only be because we know that their prayers are acceptable to God. But the more saintly is a Saint, the more acceptable is his prayer to God. Consequently we ought always to make the greater Saints our intercessors with God, and never the lesser ones.

Yet although the greater Saints are more acceptable to God than are the lesser ones, it is still useful to pray sometimes to the lesser Saints. And this for five reasons: Firstly, because a man sometimes has a greater devotion to some lesser Saint than to one who is greater; and the efficacy of our prayers depends very much on our devotion. Secondly, in order to avoid weariness; for unremitting application to one thing begets distaste; but when we pray to various Saints fresh devotional fervour is stirred up in practically each case. Thirdly, because certain Saints are appointed the patrons of certain particular cases, so S. Antony for the avoidance of hell-fire. Fourthly, that so we may show due honour to them all. Fifthly, because sometimes a favour may be gained at the prayer of many which would not be gained at the prayer of one alone.

3. Christ, even as man, is termed *the Saint of Saints*, and it belongs to Him, as man, to pray. Yet we never ask Christ to pray for us. Hence it is superfluous to make the Saints our intercessors with God.

But prayer is an act. And acts belong to individual beings. Consequently, if we were to say, *Christ, pray for us*, we should appear, unless we added something, to be referring this to Christ's Person, and thus we might seem to fall into the error of Nestorius who regarded the Person of the Son of Man as distinct in Christ from the Person of the Son of God; or perhaps, too, into the error of Arius who regarded the Person of the Son as less than the Father. In order, then, to avoid these errors, the Church does not say, *Christ, pray for us*, but *Christ, hear us*, or *Christ, have mercy on us*.

4. Once more, when one is asked to intercede for another, he presents the latter's prayers to him with whom he has to intercede. But it is superfluous to present anything to Him to Whom all things are present. Hence it is superfluous to make the Saints our intercessors with God.

But the Saints are not said to present our prayers to God as though they were manifesting to Him something which He did not know, but in the sense that they ask that these prayers may be heard by God, or that they consult the Divine Truth concerning them, so as to know what, according to His providence, ought to be done.

5. Lastly, that must be held superfluous which is done for the sake of something which, whether the former were done or not, would yet take place—or not take place—all the same. But similarly, the Saints would pray for us or not pray for us whether we asked them to do so or not. For if we deserve that they should pray for us, they would pray for us, even though we did not ask them to do so; if, on the other hand, we are not deserving that they should pray for us, then they do not pray for us—even though we ask them to do so. Hence to ask them to pray for us seems altogether superfluous.

But a man becomes deserving that some Saint should pray for him from the very fact that with pure-hearted devotion he has recourse to him in his needs. Hence it is not superfluous to pray to the Saints.

III

Are the Saints' Prayers to God for us always heard?

In 2 Maccabees xv. 14 it is said: *This is he that prayeth much for the people, and for all the Holy City, Jeremias the prophet of God*; and that his prayer was heard is evident from what follows, for *Jeremias stretched forth his right hand and gave to Judas a sword of gold, saying: Take this holy sword, a gift from God*, etc.

Further, S. Jerome says: "You say in your book that while we live we can pray for one another, but that after we are dead no one's prayer for others will be heard"; and S. Jerome condemns this statement thus: "If the Apostles and Martyrs while still in the body could pray for others while as yet solicitous for themselves, how much more when they have won their crown, completed the victory, and gained their triumph?"

Moreover, the Church's custom confirms this, for she frequently asks to be helped by the prayers of the Saints.

The Saints are said to pray for us in two ways: firstly, by express prayer, when they by their ardent desires appeal to the ears of the Divine Mercy for us; secondly, by interpretative prayer—namely, by their merits which, standing as the Saints do in the sight of God, not only tend to their own glory but are, as it were, suffrages—and even prayers—for us; just as the Blood of Christ, shed for us, is said to ask pardon for us. And in both ways the prayers of the Saints are, as far as in them lies, efficacious in obtaining what they ask for. But that we do not obtain the fruit of their prayers may be due to defects on our part, according, that is, as they are said to pray for us in the sense that their merits avail for us. But according as they actually do pray for us—that is, ask something for us by their desires—they are always heard. For the Saints only wish what God wishes, and they only ask for what they wish should be done; what God, however, wishes is always done—unless, indeed, we are speaking of the *antecedent* will of God, according to which *He wills all men to be saved*: this will is not always fulfilled. Hence it is not to be wondered at if what the Saints also will according to this kind of will is not always fulfilled.

But some maintain that the Saints' prayers for us are not always heard, thus:

1. If the Saints' prayers were always heard, they would be especially heard when they pray for those things which affect themselves. Yet they are not always heard as regards these things, for to the Martyrs who prayed for vengeance upon the inhabitants of the earth it was said *that they should rest for a little time till* the number of *their brethren should be filled up*. Much less, then, are their prayers heard for things that do not concern them.

But this prayer of the Martyrs is nothing more than their desire to obtain the garment of the body and the society of the Saints who are to be saved; it expresses their agreement with the Divine Justice which punishes the wicked. Hence on those words of the Apocalypse, *How long, O Lord*, the Ordinary Gloss says: "They yearn for a greater joy, and for the companionship of the Saints, and they agree with the justice of God."

2. It is said in Jeremias: *If Moses and Samuel shall stand before Me, My soul is not towards this people*. The Saints, then, are not always heard when they pray for us to God.

But God here speaks of Moses and Samuel according as they were in this life, for they are said to have prayed for the people and thus withstood the wrath of God. Yet none the less, had

66

they lived in Jeremias' time they would not have been able to appease by their prayers God's wrath upon the people, so great was the latter's wickedness. This is the meaning of that passage.

3. The Saints in our Fatherland are said to be the equals of the Angels. But the Angels are not always heard in their prayers to God, as is evident from Daniel: *I am come for thy words. But the Prince of the kingdom of the Persians resisted me one and twenty days.* But the Angel who spoke had not come to Daniel's assistance without asking his freedom from God; yet none the less the fulfilment of his prayer was hindered. In the same way, then, neither are the prayers of other Saints to God for us always heard.

But this contest of the good Angels is not to be understood in the sense that they put forth contrary prayers before God, but that they set before the Divine scrutiny conflicting merits on either hand, and awaited the Divine decision. Thus S. Gregory, expounding the above words of Daniel, says: "These sublime Spirits who rule over the nations in no sense strive for those who do evil, but they scrutinize their deeds and judge justly; hence, when the faults or the merits of any nation are submitted to the Council of the Supreme Court, he who is set over that particular nation is described as either losing or failing in the contest. But the sole victory for all of them is the supreme will of his Creator above him; and since they ever look towards that Will, they never desire what they cannot obtain," and hence never ask for it. Whence it is clear that their prayers are always heard.

4. Whoever obtains something by prayer in a certain sense merits it. But the Saints who are in our Fatherland are no longer capable of meriting. Therefore they cannot obtain anything for us from God by their prayers.

But although the Saints when once they are in our Fatherland are not capable of meriting for themselves, they are still capable of meriting for others, or rather of helping others by reason of their own previous merits. For when alive they merited from God that their prayers should be heard after death. Or we might say that in prayer merit and the power to obtain what we ask do not rest on the same basis. For merit consists in a certain correspondence between an act and the end towards which it is directed and which is given to it as its reward; but the impetratory power of prayer rests upon the generosity of him from whom we ask something. Consequently prayer sometimes wins from the generosity of him to whom it is made what perhaps was not merited either by him who asked nor by him for whom he asked. And thus, though the Saints are no longer capable of meriting, it does not follow that they are incapable of winning things from God.

5. Again, the Saints conform their will in all things to the Divine Will. Therefore they can only will what they know God wills. But no one prays save for what he wishes. Consequently they only pray for what they know God wills. But what God wills would take place whether they prayed or not. Consequently their prayers have no power to obtain things.

But, as is evident from the passage of S. Gregory quoted above in reply to the third difficulty, neither the Saints nor the Angels will anything save what they see in the Divine Will. And consequently they ask for nothing else save this. But it does not follow that their prayers are without fruit, for, as S. Augustine says in his treatise, *On the Predestination of the Saints*, and S. Gregory in his *Dialogues*, the prayers of the Saints avail for the predestinate, because perhaps it was pre-ordained that they should be saved by the prayers of those who interceded for them. And so, too, God wills that by the prayers of the Saints should be fulfilled what the Saints see that He wills.

6. Lastly, the prayers of the entire Court of Heaven should, if they can gain anything at all, be far more efficacious than all the suffrages of the Church on earth. But if all the suffrages of the Church on earth were to be accumulated upon one soul in Purgatory, it would be entirely freed from punishment. Since, then, the Saints who are in our Fatherland have the same reason for praying for the souls in Purgatory as they have for praying for us, they would by their prayers, if they could obtain anything for us, wholly deliver from suffering those who are in Purgatory. But this is false, for if it were true, then the suffrages of the Church for the dead would be superfluous.

But the suffrages of the Church for the dead are, as it were, satisfactions offered by the living in place of the dead, and thus they free the dead from that debt of punishment which they have not paid. But the Saints who are in our Fatherland are not capable of making satisfaction. And thus there is no parity between their prayers and the Church's suffrages.

QUESTION CLXXIX

OF THE DIVISION OF LIFE INTO THE ACTIVE AND THE CONTEMPLATIVE

I

May Life be fittingly divided into the Active and the Contemplative?

S. Gregory the Great says: "There are two kinds of lives in which Almighty God instructs us by His Sacred Word—namely, the active and the contemplative."

Those things are properly said to live which move or work from within themselves. But what especially accords with the innermost nature of a thing is that which is proper to it and towards which it is especially inclined; consequently every living thing shows that it is living by those very acts which are especially befitting it and towards which it is especially inclined. Thus the life of plants is said to consist in their growing and in their producing seed; the life of animals in their feeling and moving; while that of man consists in his understanding and in his acting according to reason.

Hence among men themselves each man's life appears to be that in which he takes special pleasure, that with which he is particularly occupied, that, in fine, in which each one wishes to live with a friend, as is said in the *Ethics of Aristotle*.

Since, then, some men are especially occupied with the contemplation of the truth while others are especially-occupied with external things, man's life may be conveniently divided into the active and the contemplative.

Some, however, repudiate this division, thus:

1. The soul is by its essence the principle of life; thus the Philosopher says: "For living things, to live is to be." But the same soul with its faculties is the principle both of action and of contemplation. Hence it would seem that life cannot be suitably divided into the active and the contemplative.

But the peculiar nature of every individual thing—that which makes it actually be—is the principle of its own proper action; consequently *to live* is said to be the very *being* of living things, and this because living things—by the very fact that they exist through such a nature— act in such a way.

2. Again, when one thing precedes another it is unfitting to divide the former by differences which find place in the latter. But action and contemplation, like speculation and practice, are distinctions in the intellect, as is laid down by the Philosopher. But we live before we understand; for life is primarily in living things by their vegetative soul, as also the Philosopher says. Therefore life is not fittingly divided according to contemplation and action.

But we do not say that life universally considered is divided into the active and the contemplative, but that man's life is so divided. For man derives his species from his intellect, hence the same divisions hold good for human life as hold good for the intellect.

3. Lastly, the word "life" implies motion, as is clear from Denis the Areopagite. But contemplation more especially consists in repose, according to the words: *When I go into my house I shall repose myself with her (Wisdom)*.

But while contemplation implies a certain repose from external occupations, it is still a certain motion of the intellect in the sense that every operation is a motion; in this sense the Philosopher says that to feel and to understand are certain motions in the sense that motion is said to be the act of a perfect thing. It is in this sense, too, that Denis assigns three movements to the soul in contemplation: the direct, the circular, and the oblique.

S. Augustine: Two virtues are set before the human soul, the one active, the other contemplative; the former shows the path, the latter shows the goal; in the one we toil that so the heart may be purified for the Vision of God, in the other we repose and we see God; the one is spent in the practice of the precepts of this temporal life, the other is occupied with the teachings of the life that is eternal. Hence it is that the one is a life of toil and the other a life of rest; for the former is engaged in purging away its sins, the latter already stands in the light of the purified. Hence, too, during this mortal life the former is occupied with the works of a good life, whereas the latter rather stands in faith, and, in the case of some few, sees *through a mirror in a dark manner*, and enjoys *in part* a certain glimpse of the Unchangeable Truth (*De Consensu Evangelistarum*, I., iv. 8).

"The Lord is the portion of my inheritance and of my cup; it is Thou that wilt restore my inheritance to me. The lines are fallen unto me in goodly places; for my inheritance is goodly to me."

S. Augustine: There is another life, the life of immortality, and in it there are no ills; there we shall see face to face what we now see *through a glass and in a dark manner* even when we have made great advance in our study of the Truth. The Church, then, knows of two kinds of life Divinely set before Her and commended to Her; in the one we walk by faith, in the other by sight; the one is the pilgrimage of time, the other is the mansion of eternity; the one is a life of toil, the other of repose; in the one we are on the way, in the other in Our Father's Home; the one is spent in the toil of action, the other in the reward of contemplation; the one *turneth away from evil and doth good*, the other hath no evil from which to turn away, but rather a Great Good Which it enjoys; the one is in conflict with the foe, the other reigns— conscious that there is no foe; the one is strong in adversity, the other knows of no adversity; the one bridles the lusts of the flesh, the other is given up to the joys of the Spirit; the one is anxious to overcome, the other is tranquil in the peace of victory; the one is helped in temptations, the other, without temptation, rejoices in its Helper; the one succours the needy, the other dwells where none are needy; the one condones the sins of others that thereby its

70

own sins may be condoned, the other suffers naught that it can pardon nor does ought that calls for pardon; the one is afflicted in sufferings lest it should be uplifted in good things, the other is steeped in such fulness of grace as to be free from all evil that so, without temptation to pride, it may cling to the Supreme Good; the one distinguishes between good and evil, the other sees naught save what is good; the one therefore is good—yet still in miseries, the other is better—and in Blessedness (*Tractatus*, cxxiv. 5, *in Joannem*).

"Jesu nostra RedemptioAmor et Desiderium!Deus Creator omnium,Homo in fine temporum!"

II

Is this division of Life into the Active and the Contemplative a sufficient one?

These two kinds of life are signified by the two wives of Jacob—namely, the active life by Lia, the contemplative by Rachel. They are also signified by those two women who afforded hospitality to the Lord: the contemplative, namely, by Mary, the active by Martha, as S. Gregory says. But if there were more than two kinds of life, these significations would not be fitting.

As we have said above, the division in question concerns human life regarded as intellectual. And the intellect itself is divided into the contemplative and the active, for the aim of intellectual knowledge is either the actual knowledge of the truth—and this belongs to the contemplative intellect, or it is some external action—and this concerns the practical or active intellect. Hence life is quite sufficiently divided into the active and the contemplative.

But some argue that this division is not a sufficient one, thus:

1. The Philosopher says that there are three specially excellent kinds of life: the pleasurable, the civil—which seems to be identified with the active—and the contemplative.

But the pleasurable life makes its end consist in the pleasures of that body which we have in common with the brute creation. Hence, as the Philosopher says in the same place, this is a bestial life. Consequently it is not comprised in our division of life into the active and the contemplative.

2. Again, S. Augustine speaks of three different kinds of life: the life of leisure, which is referred to the contemplative; the busy life, which is referred to the active life; and he adds a third composed of these two.

But things which hold a middle course are compounded of the extremes, and hence are virtually contained in them, as the tepid in the hot and the cold, the pallid in the white and the black. And similarly, under the active and the contemplative lives is comprised that kind of life which is compounded of them both. But just as in every mixture one of the simple elements predominates, so in this mixed kind of life now the contemplative, now the active predominates.

3. Lastly, men's lives are diversified according to their various occupations. But there are more than two classes of human occupations.

But all classes of human occupations are, if they are concerned with the necessities of this present life, and in accordance with right reason, comprised under the active life which, by properly regulated acts, takes heed for the needs of the present life. But if these actions minister to our concupiscences, then they fall under the voluptuous life which is not comprised in the active life. But human occupations which are directed to the consideration of the truth are comprised under the contemplative life.

S. Augustine: Your life is hid with Christ in God. When Christ shall appear, Who is your life, then you also shall appear with Him in glory; but until that shall come to pass *we see now through a glass in a dark manner*—that is, in images as it were—*but then face to face.* This, indeed, is the contemplation that is promised to us, the goal of all our actions, the eternal perfection of all our joys. For *we are the sons of God, and it hath not yet appeared what we shall be; we know that when He shall appear we shall be like Him, for we shall see Him as He is.* And as He said to His servant Moses: *I am Who am ... thus shalt thou say to the children of Israel: He Who is hath sent me to you,* even that shall we contemplate when we live in eternity. Thus, too, He says: *This is eternal life, that they may know Thee, the only True God, and Jesus Christ Whom Thou hast sent.* And this shall be when the Lord shall come and *bring to light the hidden things of darkness,* when the gloom of our mortal corruption shall have passed away. Then will be our "morning," that "morning" of which the Psalmist says: *In the morning I will stand before Thee and I will see.* ... Then, too, will come to pass that which is written: *Thou shalt fill me with joy with Thy countenance.* Beyond that joy we shall seek for nothing, for there is naught further to be sought. The Father will be shown to us, and that will suffice for us. Well did Philip understand this when he said to the Lord: *Show us the Father, and it is enough for us!* ... Such contemplation, indeed, is the reward of faith, and for this reward's sake are our hearts purified by faith, as it is written: *Purifying their hearts by faith* (*De Trinitate*, I., viii. 17).

"Remember, O Lord, Thy bowels of compassion; and Thy mercies that are from the beginning of the world. The sins of my youth and my ignorances do not remember. According to Thy mercy remember Thou me; for Thy goodness' sake, O Lord. The Lord is sweet and righteous; therefore He will give a law to sinners in the way. He will guide the mild in judgment; He will teach the meek His ways. All the ways of the Lord are mercy and truth to them that seek after His covenant and His testimonies. For Thy Name's sake, O Lord, Thou wilt pardon my sin; for it is great."

QUESTION CLXXX

OF THE CONTEMPLATIVE LIFE

I

Is the Contemplative Life wholly confined to the Intellect, or does the Will enter into it?

S. Gregory the Great says: "The contemplative life means keeping of charity towards God and our neighbour, and fixing all our desires on our Creator." But desire and love belong to the affective or appetitive powers; consequently the contemplative life is not confined to the intellect.

When men's thoughts are principally directed towards the contemplation of the truth, their life is said to be "contemplative." But to "intend" or direct is an act of the will, since "intention" or direction is concerned with the end in view, and the end is the proper object of the will. Hence contemplation, having regard to the actual essence of it, is an act of the intellect; but if we consider that which moves us to the exercise of such an act, then contemplation is an act of the will; for it is the will which moves all the other faculties, including the intellect, to the exercise of their appropriate acts.

But the appetitive faculty—the will, that is—moves us to consider some point either sensibly or intellectually, that is, sometimes out of love for the thing itself—for *Where thy treasure is there is thy heart also*,—and sometimes out of love of that very knowledge which follows from its consideration. For this reason S. Gregory makes the contemplative life consist in the love of God, since from love of God a man yearns to look upon His beauty. And since we are delighted when we obtain what we love, the contemplative life consequently results in delight, and this resides in the affective powers, from which, too, love took its rise.

Some, however, urge that the contemplative life lies wholly in the intellect, thus:

1. The Philosopher says: "The end of contemplation is truth." But truth belongs wholly to the intellect.

But from the very fact that truth is the goal of contemplation it derives its character of a desirable and lovable and pleasing good, and in this sense it comes under the appetitive powers.

2. Again, S. Gregory says: "Rachel, whose name is interpreted 'the Beginning seen,' signifies the contemplative life." But the vision of a principle, or beginning, belongs to the intellect.

But it is love of God which excites in us desire of the vision of the First Principle of all—viz., God Himself—and hence S. Gregory says: "The contemplative life, trampling underfoot all cares, ardently yearns to look upon the face of the Creator."

3. S. Gregory says: "It belongs to the contemplative life to rest from all exterior action." But the affective or appetitive powers tend towards external action. Hence it would seem that the contemplative life does not come under them.

But the appetitive powers not only move the bodily members to the performance of external acts, but the intellect, too, is moved by them to the exercise of contemplation.

"Hear, you that are far off, what I have done, and you that are near, know My strength. The sinners in Sion are afraid, trembling hath seized upon the hypocrites. Which of you can dwell with devouring fire? which of you shall dwell with everlasting burnings? He that walketh in justices, and speaketh truth, that casteth away avarice by oppression, and shaketh his hands from all bribes, that stoppeth his ears lest he hear blood, and shutteth his eyes that he may see no evil. He shall dwell on high, the fortifications of rocks shall be his highness: bread is given him, his waters are sure. His eyes shall see THE KING IN HIS BEAUTY, they shall see the land far off."

S. Thomas: We do not enjoy all the things that we have; and this is either because they do not afford us delight, or because they are not the ultimate goal of our desires, and so are incapable of satisfying our yearnings or affording us repose. But these three things the Blessed have in God: for they see Him, and seeing Him they hold Him ever present to them, for they have it in their power always to see Him; and holding Him, they enjoy Him, satisfying their yearnings with That Which is The Ultimate End (*Summa Theologica*, I., xii. 7, *ad 3m*).

"As the hart panteth after the fountains of water: so my soul panteth after Thee, O God. My soul hath thirsted after the strong living God; when shall I come and appear before the face of God? My tears have been my bread day and night, whilst it is said to me daily: Where is thy God? These things I remembered, and poured out my soul in me; for I shall go over into the place of the wonderful tabernacle, even to the house of God. With the voice of joy and praise; the noise of one feasting. Why art thou sad, O my soul? and why dost thou trouble me? Hope in God, for I will still give praise to Him: the salvation of my countenance, and my God."

II

Do the Moral Virtues pertain to the Contemplative Life?

The moral virtues are directed towards external actions, and S. Gregory says: "It belongs to the contemplative life to abstain from all external action." Hence the moral virtues do not pertain to the contemplative life.

A thing may pertain to the contemplative life either essentially or by way of disposition towards it. Essentially, then, the moral virtues do not pertain to the contemplative life; for the goal of the contemplative life is the consideration of truth. "Knowledge," says the Philosopher, "which pertains to the consideration of truth, has little to do with the moral virtues." Hence he also says that moral virtues pertain to active, not to contemplative happiness.

But dispositively the moral virtues do belong to the contemplative life. For actual contemplation, in which the contemplative life essentially consists, is impeded both by the vehemence of the passions which distract the soul from occupation with the things of the intellect, and divert it to the things of sense, and also by external disturbances. The moral virtues, however, keep down the vehemence of the passions, and check the disturbance that might arise from external occupations.

Consequently the moral virtues do pertain to the contemplative life, but by way of disposition thereto.

But some maintain that the moral virtues do pertain to the contemplative life, thus:

1. S. Gregory says: "The contemplative life means keeping charity towards God and our neighbour with our whole soul." But all the moral virtues—acts of which fall under precept—are reduced to love of God and of our neighbour; for *Love is the fulfilling of the Law.*Consequently it would seem that the moral virtues do pertain to the contemplative life.

But, as we have already said, the contemplative life is motived by the affective faculties, and consequently love of God and of our neighbour are required for the contemplative life. Impelling causes, however, do not enter into the essence of a thing, but prepare for it and perfect it. Hence it does not follow that the moral virtues essentially pertain to the contemplative life.

2. Again; the contemplative life is especially directed towards the contemplation of God, as S. Gregory says: "The soul, trampling all cares underfoot, ardently yearns to see its Creator's face." But no one can attain to this without that cleanness of heart which the moral virtues procure: *Blessed are the clean of heart, for they shall see God*, and again: *Follow peace with all men with holiness, without which no man shall see God.*

But holiness—that is, cleanness of heart—is produced by those virtues which have to do with those passions which hinder the purity of the reason. And peace is produced by justice—the moral virtue which is concerned with our works: *The work of justice shall be peace* inasmuch, that is, as a man, by refraining from injuring others, removes occasions of strife and disturbance.

3. Lastly, S. Gregory says: "The contemplative life is something beautiful in the soul," and it is for this reason that it is said to be typified by Rachel, for *She was well-favoured and of a beautiful countenance.* But the beauty of the soul, as S. Ambrose remarks, depends upon the moral virtues and especially on that of temperance.

But beauty consists in a certain splendour combined with a becoming harmony. Both of these points are radically to be referred to the reason, for to it belongs both the light which manifests beauty, and the establishment of due proportion in others. Consequently in the contemplative life—which consists in the act of the reason—beauty is necessarily and essentially to be found; thus of the contemplation of Wisdom it is said: *And I became a lover of her beauty.* But in the moral virtues beauty is only found by a certain participation—in proportion, namely, as they share in the harmony of reason; and this is especially the case with the virtue of temperance whose function it is to repress those desires which particularly obscure the light of reason. Hence it is, too, that the virtue of chastity especially renders a man fit for contemplation, for venereal pleasures are precisely those which, as S. Augustine points out, most drag down the mind to the things of sense.

S. Augustine: While it is true that any one of these three kinds of life—the leisurely, the busy, and the life commingled of them both—may be embraced by anybody without prejudice to his faith, and may be the means of leading him to his eternal reward, it is yet important that a man should take note of what it is that he holds to through love of the truth, and should reflect on the nature of the work to which he devotes himself at the demand of charity. For no man should be so addicted to leisure as for its sake to neglect his neighbour's profit; neither should any man be so devoted to the active life as to forget the thought of God. For in our leisured life we are not to find delight in mere idle repose, but the seeking and finding of the truth must be our aim; each must strive to advance in that, to hold fast what he finds, and yet not to grudge it to his neighbour. Similarly, in the life of action: we must not love honour in this life, nor power; for *all things are vain under the sun.* But we must love the toil itself which comes to us together with such honour or power if it be rightly and profitably used—as tending, that is, to the salvation under God of those under us.... Love of truth, then, seeks for a holy leisure; the calls of charity compel us to undertake the labours of justice. If no one lays on us this burden, then must we devote our leisure to the search after and the study of the truth; but if such burden be imposed upon us, we must shoulder it at the call of charity; yet withal we must not wholly abandon the delights of the truth, lest while the latter's sweetness is withdrawn from us, the burden we have taken up overwhelm us (*Of the City of God*, xix. 19).

"O expectation of Israel, the Saviour thereof in time of trouble: why wilt Thou be as a stranger in the land, and as a wayfaring man turning in to lodge? Why wilt Thou be as a wandering man, as a mighty man that cannot save? but Thou, O Lord, art among us, and Thy Name is called upon us, forsake us not."

III

Does the Contemplative Life comprise many Acts?

By "life" is here meant any work to which a man principally devotes himself. Hence if there were many acts or works in the contemplative life, it would not be one life, but several.

It must be understood that we are speaking of the contemplative life as it concerns man. And between men and Angels there is, as S. Denis says, this difference—that whereas an Angel knows the truth by one simple act of intelligence, man, on the contrary, only arrives at a knowledge of the simple truth by arguing from many premises. Hence the contemplative life has only a single act in which it finds its final perfection—namely, the contemplation of the truth—and from this one act it derives its oneness. But at the same time it has many acts by means of which it arrives at this final act. Of these various acts, some are concerned with the establishment of principles from which the mind proceeds to the contemplation of truth; others, again, are concerned with deducing from these principles that truth the knowledge of which is sought. But the ultimate act, the complement of the foregoing, is the contemplation of truth.

Some, however, maintain that many acts pertain to the contemplative life, thus:

1. Richard of S. Victor distinguishes between contemplation, meditation, and thought. But these all seem to belong to the contemplative life.

But *thought*, according to Richard of S. Victor, seems to signify the consideration of many things from which a man intends to gather some single truth. Consequently, under the term *thought* may be comprised perceptions by the senses, whereby we know certain effects—imaginations, too, as well as investigation of different phenomena by the reason; in a word, all those things which conduce to a knowledge of the truth we are in search of. At the same time, according to S. Augustine, every operation of the intellect may be termed *thought. Meditation*, again, seems to refer to the process of reasoning from principles which have to do with the truth we desire to contemplate. And *contemplation*, according to S. Bernard, means the same thing, although, according to the Philosopher, every operation of the intellect may be termed "consideration." But *contemplation* is concerned with the simple dwelling upon the truth itself. Hence Richard of S. Victor says: "*Contemplation* is the soul's clear, free, and attentive dwelling upon the truth to be perceived; *meditation* is the outlook of the soul occupied in searching for the truth; *thought* is the soul's glance, ever prone to distraction."

2. Further, the Apostle says: *But we all, beholding the glory of the Lord with open face, are transformed into the same image from glory to glory.* But this refers to the contemplative life; therefore, besides the three things already mentioned—namely, contemplation, meditation and thought,—*speculation*, too, enters into the contemplative life.

But *speculation*, as S. Augustine's Gloss has it, "is derived from *speculum*, a 'mirror,' not from *specula*, a 'watch-tower.'" To see a thing in a mirror, however, is to see a cause by an effect in which its likeness is shown; thus *speculation* seems reducible to *meditation*.

3. Again, S. Bernard says: "The first and chiefest contemplation is the marvelling at God's Majesty." But to "marvel" is, according to S. John Damascene, a species of fear. Consequently it seems that many acts belong to contemplation.

But wonderment is a species of fear arising from our learning something which it is beyond our powers to understand. Hence wonderment is an act subsequent to the contemplation of sublime truth, whereas contemplation reaches its goal in the affective powers.

4. Lastly, prayer, reading, and meditation seem to belong to the contemplative life. Devout hearing, too, belongs to it, for it is said of Mary, who is the type of the contemplative life, that *sitting at the Lord's feet, she heard His word.*

Man, however, arrives at the knowledge of truth in two ways: first of all, by receiving things from others; as regards, then, the things a man receives from God: prayer is necessary, according to the words: *I called upon God, and the spirit of Wisdom came upon me.* And as for the things he receives from men: hearing is necessary if he receive them from one who speaks, reading is necessary if it be question of what is handed down in Holy Scripture. And secondly, a man arrives at the knowledge of truth by his own personal study, and for this is required meditation.

"Uni trinoque DominoSit sempiterna gloria!Qui vitam sine terminoNobis donet in Patria!"

S. Augustine: As long, then, as *we are absent from the Lord, we walk by faith and not by sight,* whence it is said: *The just man shall live in his faith.* And this is our justice as long as we are on our pilgrimage—namely, that here now by the uprightness and perfection with which we walk we strive after that perfection and fulness of justice where, in all the glory of its beauty, will be full and perfect charity. Here we chastise our body and bring it into subjection; here we give alms by conferring benefits and forgiving offences against ourselves; and we do this with joy and from the heart, and are ever instant in prayer; and all this we do in the light of that sound doctrine by which is built up right faith, solid hope, and pure charity. This, then, is our present justice whereby we run hungering and thirsting after the perfection and fulness of justice, so that hereafter we may be filled therewith (*De Perfectione justitiæ Hominis,* viii. 18).

S. Augustine: You know, then, I think, not only how you ought to pray, but what you ought to pray for; and this not because I teach you, but because He teaches you Who has deigned to teach us all. The Life of Beatitude is what we have to seek; this we have to ask for from the Lord God. And what Beatitude means is, with many, a source of much dispute. But why should we appeal to the many and their many opinions? For pithily and truly it is said in God's Scripture: *Happy is that people whose God is the Lord!* Oh, that we may be counted amongst *that people!* Oh, that we may be enabled to contemplate Him, and may come one day to live with Him unendingly! *The end of the commandment is charity from a pure heart and a good conscience, and an unfeigned faith.* And among these three, hope stands for *a good conscience.* Faith, therefore, with hope and charity, leads to God the man who prays—that is, the man who believes, who hopes, and who desires, and who in the *Lord's Prayer* meditates what he should ask from the Lord (*Ep.* cxxx. *ad probam*).

"For my heart hath been inflamed, and my reins have been changed: and I am brought to nothing, and I knew not. I am become as a beast before Thee; and I am always with Thee. Thou hast held me by my right hand; and by Thy will Thou hast conducted me; and with glory Thou hast received me. For what have I in Heaven? and besides Thee what do I desire upon earth? For Thee my flesh and my heart hath fainted away; Thou art the God of my heart; and the God that is my portion for ever. For behold they that go far from Thee shall perish; Thou hast destroyed all them that are disloyal to Thee. But it is good for me to adhere to my God, to put my hope in the Lord God: that I may declare all Thy praises, in the gates of the daughter of Sion."

IV

Does the Contemplative Life consist solely in the Contemplation of God, or in the Consideration of other Truths as well?

S. Gregory says: "In contemplation it is the Principle—namely, God—which is sought."

A thing may come under the contemplative life in two ways: either primarily, or secondarily—that is, dispositively. Now primarily the contemplation of Divine Truth belongs to the contemplative life, since such contemplation is the goal of all human life. Hence S. Augustine says: "The contemplation of God is promised to us as the goal of all our acts and the eternal consummation of all our joys." And this will be perfect in the future life when we shall see God face to face—when, consequently, it will render us perfectly blessed. But in our present state the contemplation of Divine Truth belongs to us only imperfectly—namely, *through a glass and in a dark manner*; it causes in us now a certain commencement of beatitude, which begins here, to be continued in the future. Hence even the Philosopher makes the ultimate happiness of man consist in the contemplation of the highest intelligible truths.

But since we are led to a contemplation of God by the consideration of His Divine works—*The invisible things of God ... are clearly seen, being understood by the things that are made*—it follows also that the contemplation of the Divine works belongs in a secondary sense to the contemplative life—according, namely, as by it we are led to the knowledge of God. For this reason S. Augustine says: "In the study of created things we must not exercise a mere idle and passing curiosity, but must make them a stepping-stone to things that are immortal and that abide for ever."

Thus from what we have said it is clear that four things belong, and that in a certain sequence, to the contemplative life: firstly, the moral virtues; secondly, other acts apart from that of contemplation; thirdly, the contemplation of the Divine works; and fourthly—and this is the crown of them all—the actual contemplation of the Divine Truth.

Some, however, say that the contemplative life is not merely confined to the contemplation of God but is extended to the consideration of any truth whatsoever, thus:

1. In Ps. cxxxviii. 14 we read: *Wonderful are Thy works! My soul knoweth right well!* But the knowledge of the works of God is derived from a certain contemplation of the truth. Whence it would seem that it belongs to the contemplative life to contemplate not only the Divine Truth, but also any other truth we please.

But David sought the knowledge of God's works that he might thereby be led to God Himself, as he says elsewhere: *I meditated on all Thy works, I mused upon the works of Thy hands; I stretched forth my hands to Thee.*

2. Again, S. Bernard says: "The first point in contemplation is to marvel at God's majesty; the second, at His judgments; the third, at His benefits; the fourth, at His promises." But of these only the first comes under the Divine Truth—the rest are effects of it.

But from the consideration of the Divine judgments a man is led to the contemplation of the Divine justice; and from a consideration of the Divine benefits and promises a man is led to a knowledge of the Divine mercy and goodness, as it were by effects either already shown or to be shown.

3. Once more, Richard of S. Victor distinguishes six kinds of contemplation; the first is according to the imagination simply, when, namely, we consider corporeal things; the second is in the imagination directed by the reason, as when we consider the harmony and arrangement of the things of the senses; the third is in the reason, but based on the imagination, as when by the consideration of visible things we are uplifted to the invisible; the fourth is in the reason working on the things of the reason, as when the soul occupies itself with invisible things unknown to the imagination; the fifth is above the reason, but not beyond its grasp, when, for instance, we know by Divine Revelation things which cannot be comprehended by the human reason; and the sixth is above the reason and beyond its grasp, as when by Divine illumination we know things which are apparently repugnant to human reason—for example, the things we are told concerning the mystery of the Holy Trinity.

And only the last named of these seems to come under Divine Truth; consequently contemplation of the truth is not limited to Divine Truth, but extends also to those truths which we consider in created things.

But by these six are signified the steps by which we ascend through created things to the contemplation of God. For in the first we have the perception of the things of sense; in the second, the progress from the things of sense to the things of the intellect; in the third judgment upon the things of sense according to intellectual principles; in the fourth, the simple consideration of intellectual truths at which we have arrived by means of the things of sense; in the fifth, the contemplation of intellectual truths to which we could not attain by the things of sense, but which can be grasped by reason; in the sixth, the contemplation of intellectual truths such as the reason can neither find nor grasp—truths, namely, which belong to the sublime contemplation of the Divine Truth, in which contemplation is finally perfected.

4. Lastly, in the contemplative life the contemplation of truth is sought as being man's perfection. But any truth whatsoever is a perfection of the human intellect. Consequently the contemplative life consists in the contemplation of any kind of truth whatsoever.

But the ultimate perfection of the human intellect is the Divine Truth; other truths perfect the intellect by way of preparation for the Divine Truth.

S. Augustine: Martha, Martha, thou hast chosen a good part, but Mary hath chosen the better. Yours is good—for it is good to busy oneself with waiting on the Saints—but hers is better. What you have chosen will pass away at length. You minister to the hungry, you minister to the thirsty, you make the beds for them that would sleep, you find house-room for them that need it—but all these things will pass away! For there will come a time when none will hunger, when none will thirst, when none will sleep. And then thy care will be taken from thee. But Mary hath chosen the better part, which shall never be taken from her! It shall not be taken away, for she chose to live the life of contemplation, she chose to live by the Word. What kind of life will that be that flows from the Word without spoken word? Here on earth she drew life from the Word, but through the medium of the spoken word. Then will be life, from the Word indeed, but with no spoken word. For the Word Himself is life. *We shall be like Him, for we shall see Him as He is* (*Sermon*, CLXIX., xiv. 17).

S. Augustine: One thing I have asked of the Lord, this will I seek after: that I may dwell in the house of the Lord all the days of my life!

Whosoever asks for This One Thing and seeks after It prays with sure and certain confidence; nor need he fear lest, when he shall have obtained It, he shall find It disagreeable to him, for without It naught that he prays for as he ought, and obtains, is of any avail. For this is the one, true, and only Blessed Life—to contemplate the delights of the Lord for eternity, in immortality and incorruptibility of body as well as soul. For the sake of This One Thing are all other things to be sought after, and only thus our petitions for them are rendered not unbecoming. Whosoever hath this One Thing will have all that he wishes for, nor indeed will he be able to wish there for anything which is unfitting. For there is the Fountain of Life, for which we must now thirst in prayer as long as we live by hope—as long, too, as we see not What we hope for. For we dwell 'neath the shadow of His wings before Whom is all our desire, that so we *may be inebriated with the plenty of* His *house, and may drink of the torrent of* His *pleasure: for with* Him *is the Fountain of Life, and in* His *light we shall see light.* Then shall our desire be sated with all good things, then will there be naught for us to seek for with groanings, but only What we shall cling to with joy. Yet none the less, since this is *the peace that surpasseth all understanding,* even when praying for it *we know not what we should pray for as we ought* (*Ep.* cxxx. *ad probam*).

"He shall cast death down headlong for ever: and the Lord God shall wipe away tears from every face, and the reproach of His people He shall take away from off the whole earth: for the Lord hath spoken it. And they shall say in that day: Lo, this is our God, we have waited for Him, and He will save us: this is the Lord, we have patiently waited for Him, we shall rejoice and be joyful in His salvation."

V

Can the Contemplative Life attain, according to the State of this Present Life, to the Contemplation of the Divine Essence?

S. Gregory says: "As long as we live in this mortal flesh none of us can make such progress in the virtue of contemplation as to fix his mind's gaze on that Infinite Light."

S. Augustine also says: "No one who looks on God lives with that life with which we mortals live in the bodily senses; but unless he be in some sort dead to this life, whether as having wholly departed from the body, or as rapt away from the bodily senses, he is not uplifted to that vision."

A man, then, can be "in this life" in two ways: he can be in it actually—that is, as actually using his bodily senses—and when he is thus "in the body" no contemplation such as belongs to this present life can attain to the vision of the Essence of God; or a man may be "in this life" potentially, and not actually; that is, his soul may be joined to his body as its informing principle, but in such fashion that it neither makes use of the bodily senses nor even of the imagination, and this is what takes place when a man is rapt in ecstasy: in this sense contemplation such as belongs to this life can attain to the vision of the Divine Essence.

Consequently the highest degree of contemplation which is compatible with the present life is that which S. Paul had when he was rapt in ecstasy and stood midway between the state of this present life and the next.

Some, however, say that the contemplative life can, even according to our present state of life, attain to the vision of the Divine Essence, thus:

1. Jacob said: *I have seen God face to face, and my soul hath been saved.* But the vision of the face of God is the vision of the Divine Essence. Whence it would seem that a man may by contemplation actually reach, even during this present life, to the vision of the Essence of God.

But S. Denis says: "If anyone saw God and understood what he saw, then it was not God he saw, but something belonging to Him." And similarly S. Gregory says: "Almighty God is never seen in His Glory, but the soul gazes at something derived from It, and thus refreshed, makes advance, and so ultimately arrives at the glory of vision." Hence when Jacob said, *I saw God face to face*, we are not to understand that he saw the Essence of God, but that he saw some appearance—that is, some imaginary appearance—in which God spoke to him; or, as the Gloss of S. Gregory has it, "Since we know people by the face, Jacob called knowledge of God His face."

2. Further, S. Gregory says: "Contemplative men turn back within upon themselves in that they search into spiritual things, and do not carry with them the shadows of things corporeal; or if perchance they touch them, they drive them away with discreet hands. But when they would look upon the Infinite Light, they put aside all images which limit It, and in striving to arrive at a height superior to themselves, they become conquerors of their nature." But a man is only withheld from the vision of the Divine Essence, which is Infinite Light, by the necessity he is under of turning to corporeal images. From this it would seem that contemplation can, even in this present life, arrive at the sight of the Infinite Essential Light.

But human contemplation according to this present state cannot exist without recourse to the imagination, for it is in accordance with man's nature that he should see intelligible forms through the medium of pictures in the imagination, as also the Philosopher teaches. Yet intellectual knowledge does not consist in such images, rather does the intellect contemplate in them the purity of intelligible truth; and this is not merely the case in natural knowledge, but also in those things which we know by revelation. For S. Denis says: "The Divine Light manifests to us the Angelic hierarchies by means of symbolical figures by force of which we are restored to the simple ray," that is, to the simple knowledge of intelligible truth. It is thus that we ought to understand S. Gregory's words when he says: "In contemplation men do not carry with them the shadows of things corporeal," for their contemplation does not abide in these things but rather in the consideration of intelligible truth.

3. Lastly, S. Gregory says: "To the soul that looks upon its Creator all created things are but narrow. Consequently the man of God—namely, the Blessed Benedict—who saw in a tower a fiery globe and the Angels mounting up to Heaven, was doubtless only able to see these things by the light of God." But the Blessed Benedict was then still in this life. Consequently contemplation, even in this present life, can attain to the vision of the Essence of God.

But we are not to understand from S. Gregory's words that the Blessed Benedict saw the Essence of God in that vision; S. Gregory wishes to show that since "to him who looks upon his Creator all created things are but as nothing," it follows that certain things can easily be seen by the illumination afforded by the Divine Light. Hence he adds: "For, however little of the Creator's Light he sees, all created things become of small account."

Veni Sancte SpiritusEt emitte coelitusLucis Tuæ radium!

O Lux BeatissimaReple cordis intimaTuorum fidelium!

S. Augustine: And thus, the remaining burden of this mortal life being laid aside at death, man's happiness will, in God's own time, be perfected from every point of view—that happiness which is begun in this life, and to the attainment and securing of which at some future time our every effort must now tend (*Of the Sermon on the Mount*, II., ix. 35).

"The old error is passed away; Thou wilt keep peace: peace, because we have hoped in Thee. You have hoped in the Lord for evermore, in the Lord God mighty for ever. And in the way of Thy judgments, O Lord, we have patiently waited for Thee: Thy Name, and Thy remembrance are the desire of the soul. My soul hath desired Thee in the night: yea, and with my spirit within me in the morning early I will watch to Thee."

VI

Is the Act of Contemplation Rightly Distinguished According to the Three Kinds of Motion— Circular, Direct, and Oblique?

S. Denis the Areopagite does so distinguish the acts of contemplation.

The operation of the intellect in which contemplation essentially consists is termed "motion" in the sense that motion is the act of a perfect thing, according to the Philosopher. And since we arrive at a knowledge of intelligible things through the medium of the things of sense, and the operations of the senses do not take place without motion, it follows that the operations also of the intellect are correctly described as a species of motion, and are differentiated according to the analogy of divers motions. But the more perfect and the chiefest of bodily motions are local motions, as is proved by the Philosopher. Consequently the chief intellectual motions are described according to the analogy of these latter.

Now, there are three species of local motion: one is circular, according as a thing is moved uniformly about the same centre; another is direct, according as a thing proceeds from one point to another; and a third is oblique, compounded as it were from the two foregoing.

Hence in intelligible operations, that which simply has uniformity is attributed to circular motion; that intellectual motion by which a man proceeds from one thing to another is attributed to direct motion; while that intellectual operation which has a certain uniformity combined with progress towards different points, is attributed to oblique motion.

All, however, do not agree with this division, thus:

1. Contemplation means a state of repose, as is said in *Wisdom*: *When I go into my house I shall repose myself with Her*. And motion is opposed to repose. Consequently the operations of the contemplative life cannot be designated according to these different species of motion.

But whereas external bodily movements are opposed to that repose of contemplation which is understood to be rest from external occupations, the motion of intellectual operations belongs precisely to the repose of contemplation.

2. Again, the action of the contemplative life pertains to the intellect wherein man is at one with the Angels. But S. Denis does not apply these motions to the Angels in the same way as he does to the soul; for he says that the *circular* motion of the Angels "corresponds to the illumination of the beautiful and the good." But of the *circular* motion of the soul he gives several definitions, of which the first is "the return of the soul upon itself as opposed to external things"; the second is "a certain wrapping together of the powers of the soul whereby it is freed from error and from external occupation"; and the third is "the union of the soul with things superior to it." Similarly, he speaks in different terms of the *direct* motion of the soul as compared with that of the Angels. For he says that the *direct* motion of an Angel is "according as he proceeds to the care of the things subject to him"; while the *direct* motion of the soul is made to consist in two things: first of all "that it proceeds to those things which are around it"; secondly, that "from external things it is uplifted to simple contemplation." And lastly, he explains the *oblique* motion differently in each case. For he makes the *oblique* motion of the Angels consist in this that, "while providing for those that have less than themselves, they remain in the same attitude towards God"; but the *oblique* motion of the soul he explains as meaning that "the soul is illumined by Divine knowledge rationally and diffusely."

Consequently it does not appear that the operations of contemplation are fittingly distinguished according to the aforesaid species of motion.

But while man's intellect is generally the same with that of the Angels, the intellectual powers of the latter are far higher than in man. It was therefore necessary to assign the aforesaid motions to human souls and to the Angels in different fashion in proportion as their intellectual powers are not uniform. For the Angelic intellect has uniform knowledge in two respects: firstly, because the Angels do not acquire intelligible truth from the variety of compound things; and secondly, because they do not understand intelligible truth discursively, but by simple intuition. Whereas the intellect of the human soul, on the contrary, acquires intelligible truth from the things of sense, and understands it by the discursive action of the reason.

Hence S. Denis assigns to the Angels circular motion in that they uniformly and unceasingly, without beginning or end, gaze upon God; just as circular motion, which has neither beginning nor end, is uniformly maintained round the same central point. But in the case of the human soul, its twofold lack of uniformity must be removed before it can attain to the above-mentioned uniformity. For there must first be removed that lack of uniformity which arises from the diversity of external things: that is, the soul must quit external things. And this S. Denis expresses first of all in his definition of the circular motion of the soul when he speaks of "the return of the soul upon itself as opposed to external things." And there must be removed in the second place that second lack of uniformity which arises from the discursive action of the reason. And this takes place when all the operations of the soul are reduced to the simple contemplation of intelligible truth. This forms the second part of S. Denis's definition of this circular motion—namely, when he speaks of the necessity of "a certain wrapping together of the powers of the soul," with the result that, when discursive action thus ceases, the soul's gaze is fixed on the contemplation of the one simple truth. And in this operation of the soul there is no room for error, just as there is no room for error in our understanding of first principles which we know by simple intuition.

Then, when these first two steps have been taken, S. Denis puts in the third place that uniformity, like to that of the Angels, by which the soul, laying aside all else, persists in the simple contemplation of God. And this he expresses when he says: "Then, as now made uniform, it, as a whole"—that is, as conformed (to God)—"is, with all its powers unified, led by the hand to the Beautiful and the Good."

But the *direct* motion in the Angels cannot be understood in the sense that, by considering, they proceed from one point to another; but solely according to the order of their providential care for others—according, namely, as the superior Angels illumine the inferior through those who stand between. And this is what S. Denis means when he says that the *direct* motion of an Angel is "according as he proceeds to the care of the things subject to him, taking in his course all things that are direct" following—that is, those things which are disposed in direct order. But to the human soul S. Denis assigns *direct* motion in the sense that it proceeds from the exterior things of sense to the knowledge of intelligible things.

And he assigns *oblique* motion to the Angels—a motion, that is, compounded of the *direct* and the *circular*—inasmuch as an Angel, according to his contemplation of God, provides for those inferior to him. To the human soul, on the contrary, he assigns this same *oblique* motion, similarly compounded of the *direct* and the *circular* motions, inasmuch as in its reasonings it makes use of the Divine illuminations.

3. Lastly, Richard of S. Victor gives many other and different kinds of motion. For, following the analogy of the birds of the air, he says of these latter that "some at one time ascend on high, at another swoop down to earth, and they do this again and again; others turn now to the right, now to the left, and this repeatedly; others go in advance, others fall behind; some sail round and round in circles, now narrower and now wider; while others again remain almost immovably suspended in one place." From all which it would seem that there are not merely three movements in contemplation.

But all these diversities of motion which are expressed by, up and down, to right and left, backwards and forwards, and in varying circles, are reducible either to *direct* or to *oblique* motion, for they all signify the discursive action of the reason. For if this discursive action be from the genus to the species or from the whole to the part, it will be, as Richard of S. Victor himself explains, motion upwards and downwards. If, again, it means argumentation from one thing to its opposite, it will come under motion to right and left. Or if it be deduction from cause to effect, then it will be motion backwards and forwards. And finally, if it mean arguing from the accidents which surround a thing, whether nearly or remotely, it will be circuitous motion. But the discursive action of the reason arguing from the things of sense to intelligible things according to the orderly progress of the natural reason, belongs to *direct* motion. When, however, it arises from Divine illuminations, it comes under *oblique* motion, as we have already said (in the reply to the second argument). Lastly, only the immobility which he mentions will come under *circular* motion.

Whence it appears that S. Denis has quite sufficiently, and with exceeding subtlety, described the movements of contemplation.

"For behold my witness is in Heaven, and He that knoweth my conscience is on high. For behold short years pass away, and I am walking in a path by which I shall not return."

VII

Has Contemplation its Joys?

In Wisdom viii. 16 we read: *Her conversation hath no bitterness, nor Her company any tediousness, but joy and gladness.* And S. Gregory says: "The contemplative life means a truly lovable sweetness."

There are two sources of pleasure in contemplation; for, firstly, there is the very act of contemplating, and everyone finds a certain pleasure in the performance of acts which are appropriate to his nature or to his habits. And the contemplation of truth is natural to man as a rational animal; hence it is that "all men naturally desire to know," and consequently find a pleasure in the knowledge of truth. And this pleasure is enhanced according as a man has habits of wisdom and knowledge which enable him to indulge in contemplation without difficulty.

Secondly, contemplation is pleasurable owing to the object which we contemplate, as when a man looks at something which he loves. And this holds good of even bodily vision, for not only is the mere exercise of the visual faculties pleasurable, but the seeing people whom we love is pleasurable.

Since, then, the contemplative life especially consists in the contemplation of God, to which contemplation we are moved by charity, it follows that the contemplative life is not merely pleasurable by reason of the simple act of contemplating, but also by reason of Divine Love Itself. And in both these respects the delights of contemplation exceed all other human delights. For on the one hand spiritual delights are superior to carnal delights; and on the other hand, the love of Divine charity wherewith we love God exceeds all other love; whence it is said in the Psalm: *Taste and see that the Lord is sweet.*

Some maintain, however, that contemplation is not pleasurable, thus:

1. Pleasure belongs to the appetitive powers, whereas contemplation is mainly in the intellect.

But while the contemplative life mainly consists in the intellect, it derives its principle from the affective powers, since a man is moved to contemplation by love of God. And since the end corresponds to the principle, it follows that the goal and term of the contemplative life is in the affective powers, in the sense, namely, that a man finds a pleasure in the sight of a thing which he loves, and this very pleasure stirs up in him a yet greater love. Hence S. Gregory says: "When a man sees one whom he loves his love is yet more enkindled." And in this lies the full perfection of the contemplative life: that the Divine Truth should not only be seen but loved.

2. Again, strife and contention hinder delight. But in contemplation there is strife and contention, for S. Gregory says: "The soul, when it strives after the contemplation of God, finds itself engaged in a species of combat; at one time it seems to prevail, for by understanding and by feeling it tastes somewhat of the Infinite Light; at other times it is overwhelmed, for when it has tasted it faints."

It is true indeed that contest and strife arising from the opposition presented by external things prevent us from finding pleasure in those same things. For no man finds a pleasure in the things against which he fights. But he does find a pleasure, other things being equal, in the actual attainment of a thing for which he has striven; thus S. Augustine says: "The greater the danger in the battle, the greater the joy in the triumph." And in contemplation the strife and the combat do not arise from any opposition on the part of the truth which we contemplate, but from our deficient understanding and from the corruptible nature of our bodies which ever draw us down to things beneath us: *The corruptible body is a load upon the soul, and the earthly habitation presseth down the mind that museth upon many things.* Hence it is that when a man attains to the contemplation of truth he loves it still more ardently; but at the same time he more than ever hates his own defects and the sluggishness of his corruptible body, so that with the Apostle he cries out: *Unhappy man that I am! Who shall deliver me from the body of this death?* Hence, too, S. Gregory says: "When God is known by our desires and our understanding, He causes all pleasures of the flesh to wither up within us."

3. But again, delight follows upon a perfect work. But contemplation on this earth is imperfect, according to the words of the Apostle: *We see now through a glass in a dark manner.* Hence it would seem that the contemplative life does not afford delight.

It is indeed true that the contemplation of God during this life is imperfect compared with our contemplation of Him in our eternal home; and in the same way it is true that the delights of contemplation here on earth are imperfect compared with the delights of contemplation in that home, of which latter joys the Psalmist says: *Thou shalt make them drink of the torrent of Thy pleasure.* Yet, none the less, the contemplation of Divine things here on earth is, although imperfect, far more perfect than any other subject of contemplation howsoever perfect it may be, and this by reason of the excellence of what we contemplate. Whence the Philosopher says: "It may indeed be the case that with regard to such noble existences and Divine substances we have to be content with insignificant theories, yet even though we but barely touch upon them, none the less so ennobling is such knowledge that it affords us greater delight than any other which is accessible to us." Hence, too, S. Gregory says: "The contemplative life has its most desirable sweetness which uplifts the soul above itself, opens the way to heavenly things, and makes spiritual things plain to the eyes of the soul."

4. Lastly, bodily injuries are a hindrance to delight. But contemplation is productive of bodily injuries, for we read in Genesis that Jacob, after saying *I have seen God face to face, ... halted on his foot ... because He touched the sinew of his thigh and it shrank.* Whence it would seem that the contemplative life is not pleasurable.

But after that contemplation Jacob halted on one foot because, as S. Gregory says, "it must needs be that as the love of this world grows weaker, so a man grows stronger in his love of God," and consequently, "when once we have known the sweetness of God, one of our feet remains sound while the other halts; for a man who halts with one foot leans only on the one that is sound."

"Tu esto nostrum gaudiumQui es futurus Præmium.Sit nostra in Te gloriaPer cuncta semper sæcula!"

S. Gregory: Between the delights of the body and those of the heart there is ever this difference that the delights of the body are wont, when we have them not, to beget a keen yearning for them; but when we have them and eat our fill, they straightway beget disgust for them, for we are sated therewith. Spiritual joys, on the contrary, when we have them not are a weariness, but when we have them we desire them still more, and the more we feed upon them the more we hunger after them. In the case of the former, the yearning for them was a pleasure, trial of them brought disgust. In the case of the latter, in desire we held them cheap, trial of them proved a source of pleasure. For spiritual joys increase the soul's desire of them even while they sate us, for the more their savour is perceived, the more we know what it is we ought eagerly to love. Whence it comes to pass that when we have them not we cannot love them, for their savour is unknown to us. For how can a man love what he is ignorant of? Wherefore the Psalmist admonishes us, saying: *O taste and see that the Lord is sweet!* As though he would say to us in plain terms: You know not His sweetness if ye have never tasted it; touch, then, the Food of Life with the palate of your soul that so, making proof of Its sweetness, ye may be able to love It.

These joys man lost when he sinned in Paradise; he went out when he closed his mouth to the Food of Eternal Sweetness. Whence we too, who are born amidst the toils of this pilgrimage, come without relish to this Food; we know not what we ought to desire, and the sickness of our disgust grows the more the further our souls keep away from feeding upon that Sweetness; and less and less does our soul desire those interior joys the longer it has grown accustomed to do without them. We sicken, then, by reason of our very disgust, and we are wearied by the long-drawn sickness of our hunger (*Hom.* XXXVI., *On the Gospels*).

VIII

Is the Contemplative Life lasting?

The Lord said *Mary hath chosen the best part which shall not be taken away from her* because, as S. Gregory says: "Contemplation begins here below that it may be perfected in our heavenly home."

A thing may be termed "lasting" in two ways: from its very nature, or as far as we are concerned. As far as its nature is concerned, the contemplative life is lasting in two ways: for first of all it is concerned with incorruptible and unchangeable things, and in the second place there is nothing which is its contrary: for, as Aristotle says: "To the pleasure which is derived from thought there is no contrary."

And also as far as we are concerned the contemplative life is lasting; and this both because it comes under the action of the incorruptible portion of our soul—namely, our intellect—and so can last after this life; and also because in the work of the contemplative life there is no bodily toil, and we can consequently apply ourselves more continuously to such work, as also the Philosopher remarks.

Some, however, argue that the contemplative life is not lasting, thus:

1. The contemplative life essentially concerns the intellect. But all the intellectual perfections of this life will be *made void*, as we read: *Whether prophecies shall be made void, or tongues shall cease, or knowledge shall be destroyed.*

But the fashion of contemplation here and in our Father's home is not the same; and the contemplative life is said "to last" by reason of charity, which is both its principle and its end; wherefore S. Gregory says: "The contemplative life begins here below that it may be perfected in our heavenly home, for the fire of love which begins to burn here below, when it sees Him Whom it loves, burns yet more strongly with love of Him."

2. Again, men but taste the sweetness of contemplation here, snatching at it, as it were, and in passing: whence S. Augustine says: "Thou introducest me to a most unwonted affection within me, to an unspeakable sweetness; yet I fall back again as though dragged down by a grievous weight!" And S. Gregory, expounding those words of Job, *When a spirit passed before me*, says: "The mind does not long remain steadfastly occupied with the sweetness of intimate contemplation, for it is recalled to itself, stricken back by the immensity of that Light." The contemplative life, then, is not lasting.

It is true indeed that no action can remain long at the pitch of its intensity. And the goal of contemplation is to attain to the uniformity of Divine contemplation, as Denis the Areopagite says. Hence, although in this sense contemplation cannot last long, yet it can last long as regards its other acts.

3. Lastly, what is not natural to a man cannot be lasting. "But the contemplative life," as the Philosopher says, "is beyond man."

But the Philosopher says that the contemplative life is "beyond man" in the sense that it belongs to us according to what is Divine in us—namely, our intellect; for our intellect is incorruptible and impassible in itself, and consequently its action can be more lasting.

S. Augustine: This day sets before us the great mystery of our eternal beatitude. For that life which this day signifies will not pass away as to-day is to pass away. Wherefore, brethren, we exhort and beseech you by the Name of our Lord Jesus Christ by Whom our sins are forgiven, by Him Who willed that His Blood should be our ransom, by Him Who has deigned that we who are not deserving to be called His slaves should yet be called His brethren—we beseech you that your entire aim, that which gives you your very name of "Christian," and by reason of which you bear His Name upon your foreheads and in your hearts, may be directed solely to that life which we are to share with the Angels; that life where is to be unending repose, everlasting joy, unfailing happiness, rest without disturbance, joy without sadness, no death. What that life is none can know save those who have made trial of it; and none can make trial of it save those who have faith (*Sermon*, CCLIX., *On Low Sunday*).

"And thou shalt say in that day: I will give thanks to Thee, O Lord, for Thou wast angry with me: Thy wrath is turned away, and Thou hast comforted me. Behold, God is my Saviour. I will deal confidently, and will not fear: because the Lord is my strength, and my praise, and He is become my salvation. You shall draw waters with joy out of the Saviour's fountains: And you shall say in that day: Praise ye the Lord, and call upon His Name: make His works known among the people: remember that His Name is high. Sing ye to the Lord, for He hath done great things: shew this forth in all the earth. Rejoice, and praise, O thou habitation of Sion: for great is He that is in the midst of thee, the holy One of Israel."

QUESTION CLXXXI

OF THE ACTIVE LIFE

I

Do all Acts of the Moral Virtues come under the Active Life?

S. Isidore says: "In the active life all the vices are first of all to be removed by the practice of good works, so that in the contemplative life a man may, with now purified mental gaze, pass to the contemplation of the Divine Light." But all the vices can only be removed by the acts of the moral virtues. Consequently the acts of the moral virtues belong to the active life.

As we have said already, the active and the contemplative lives are distinguished by the different occupations of men who are aiming at different ends, one being the consideration of Truth—the goal of the contemplative life; the other external works with which the active life is occupied. But it is clear that the moral virtues are not especially concerned with the contemplation of truth but with action; thus the Philosopher says: "For virtue, knowledge is of little or no avail." It is therefore manifest that the moral virtues essentially belong to the active life; and in accordance with this the Philosopher refers the moral virtues to active happiness.

Some, however, maintain that all the acts of the moral virtues do not belong to the active life, thus:

1. The active life seems to consist solely in those things which have to do with our neighbour; for S. Gregory says: "The active life means breaking bread to the hungry;" and at the close, after enumerating many things which have to do with our neighbour, he adds: "And to provide for each according as they have need." But not by all the acts of the moral virtues are we brought into contact with others, but only by justice and its divisions. Consequently all the acts of the moral virtues do not belong to the active life.

But the chief of the moral virtues is justice, and by it a man is brought into contact with his neighbour, as the Philosopher proves. We describe, then, the active life by those things by means of which we are brought into contact with our neighbour; yet we do not thereby mean that the active life consists solely in these things, but chiefly in them.

2. Again, S. Gregory says: "By Lia, who was blear-eyed but fruitful, is signified the active life which sees less clearly, since occupied with works; but when, now by word, now by example, it arouses its neighbour to imitation, it brings forth many children in good works." But all this seems rather to come under charity, by which we love our neighbour, than under the moral virtues. Consequently the acts of the moral virtues seem not to belong to the active life.

But a man can, by acts of all the moral virtues, lead his neighbour to good works by his example; and this S. Gregory here attributes to the active life.

3. Lastly, the moral virtues dispose us to the contemplative life. But disposition to a thing and the perfect attainment of that thing come under the same head. Consequently the moral virtues do not belong to the active life.

But just as a virtue which is directed towards the end of another virtue passes over, in some sort, into the species of that latter virtue, so also when a man uses those things which belong to the active life precisely as disposing him to contemplation, then those things which he so uses are comprised under the contemplative life. But for those who devote themselves to the works of the moral virtues as being good in themselves and not as dispositive towards the contemplative life, the moral virtues belong to the active life. Although at the same time it might be said that the active life is a disposition to the contemplative life.

"O death, how bitter is the remembrance of thee to a man that hath peace in his possessions, to a man that is at rest, and whose ways are prosperous in all things, and that is yet able to take meat! O death, thy sentence is welcome to the man that is in need, and to him whose strength faileth, who is in a decrepit age, and that is in care about all things, and to the distrustful that loseth patience! Fear not the sentence of death. Remember what things have been before thee, and what shall come after thee: this sentence is from the Lord upon all flesh. And what shall come upon thee by the good pleasure of the Most High whether ten, or a hundred, or a thousand years."

II

Does Prudence pertain to the Active Life?

The Philosopher says that prudence pertains to active happiness, and to this pertain the moral virtues.

As we have said above, when one thing is directed towards the attainment of another thing as its end, it—and this especially holds good in morals—is, so to speak, drawn into the species of that towards which it is thus directed, thus: "He who commits adultery in order to steal" says the Philosopher, "is rather a thief than an adulterer." Now it is clear that that knowledge which is prudence is directed to the acts of the moral virtues as its end, for prudence is "the right mode of procedure in our actions;" hence, too, the ends of the moral virtues are the principles of prudence, as the Philosopher also says in the same work. In the same way, then, as we said above that in the case of a man who directs them to the repose of contemplation, the moral virtues pertain to the contemplative life, so also the knowledge which is prudence, and which is by its very nature directed to the operations of the moral virtues, directly pertains to the active life—that is, of course, on the supposition that prudence is understood in the strict sense in which the Philosopher speaks of it. If, however, prudence be understood in a broad sense—namely, as embracing all kinds of human knowledge—then prudence pertains, at least in certain of its aspects, to the contemplative life; thus Cicero says: "The man who can see a truth the most clearly and quickly, and explain the reason of it, is rightly regarded as most prudent and most wise."

But some maintain that prudence does not pertain to the active life, thus:

1. Just as the contemplative life pertains to the cognoscitive powers, so does the active life pertain to the appetitive powers. But prudence does not pertain to the appetitive powers but rather to the cognoscitive. Consequently it does not pertain to the active life.

But moral acts derive their character from the end towards which they are directed; consequently to the contemplative life belongs that kind of knowledge which makes its end consist in the very knowledge of truth. But the knowledge which is prudence, and which is rather directed to the acts of the appetitive powers, pertains to the active life.

2. Again, S. Gregory says "The active life, occupied as it is with works, sees less clearly," and hence is typified by Lia, who was blear-eyed. But prudence demands clear vision, so that a man may judge what is to be done. Whence it would seem that prudence does not pertain to the active life.

But occupation with external things only makes a man see less clearly those intelligible truths which are not connected with the things of sense; the external occupations of the active life, however, make a man see more clearly in his judgment on a course of action—and this is a question of prudence—for he has experience, and his mind is attentive: "When you are attentive," says Sallust, "then mental acumen avails."

3. Lastly, prudence comes midway betwixt the moral and the intellectual virtues. But just as the moral virtues pertain to the active life, so do the intellectual virtues pertain to the contemplative. Hence it would seem that prudence belongs neither to the active nor to the contemplative life, but, as S. Augustine says, to a kind of life which is betwixt and between. But prudence is said to come betwixt the intellectual and the moral virtues in the sense that, whereas it has the same subject as the intellectual virtues, it yet coincides as regards its object with the moral virtues. And that third species of life comes betwixt and between the active and the contemplative life as regards the things with which it is concerned, for at one time it is occupied with the contemplation of truth, at another time with external matters.

"For what shall I do when God shall rise to judge? and when He shall examine, what shall I answer Him? For I have always feared God as waves swelling over me, and His weight I was not able to bear."

III

Does Teaching Belong to the Active or to the Contemplative Life?

S. Gregory says: "The active life means breaking bread to the hungry; teaching words of wisdom to them that know them not."

The act of teaching has a twofold object: for teaching is by speaking, and speaking is the audible sign of an interior mental concept. One object, therefore, of our teaching is the matter to be taught, the object, that is, of our interior concepts; and in this sense teaching sometimes belongs to the active, sometimes to the contemplative life. It belongs to the active life if a man forms interiorly some concept of a truth with a view to thus directing his external acts; but it belongs to the contemplative life if a man interiorly conceives some intelligible truth and delights in the thought of it and the love of it. Whence S. Augustine says: "Let them choose for themselves the better part—that, namely, of the contemplative life; let them devote themselves to the Word of God; let them yearn for the sweetness of teaching; let them occupy themselves with the knowledge that leads to salvation"—where he clearly says that teaching belongs to the contemplative life.

The second object of teaching arises from the fact that teaching is given through the medium of audible speech and thus the hearer himself is the object of the teaching; and from this point of view all teaching belongs to the active life to which pertain all external actions.

Some, however, regard teaching as rather belonging to the contemplative than to the active life, thus:

1. S. Gregory says: "Perfect men declare to their brethren those good things of Heaven which they themselves have been able to contemplate at least 'through a glass,' and they thus kindle in their hearts the love of that hidden beauty." Yet what is this but teaching? To teach, therefore, is an act of the contemplative life.

But S. Gregory expressly speaks here of teaching from the point of view of the matter that is presented—that is, of teaching as it is concerned with the consideration of and love of the truth.

2. Again, acts and habits seem to belong to the same kind of life. But to teach is an act of wisdom, for the Philosopher says: "The proof that a man knows is that he is able to teach." Since, then, wisdom—that is, knowledge—pertains to the contemplative life, it would seem that teaching also must pertain to the contemplative life.

But habits and acts agree in their object, and consequently the argument just given is based upon the material of the interior concept. For the capacity for teaching is possessed by a wise or learned man just in proportion as he can express in outward words the concepts of his mind and so be able to bring home a truth to someone else.

3. Lastly, prayer is an act of the contemplative life just in the same way as is contemplation itself. But prayer, even when one man prays for another, belongs to the contemplative life. Hence it would seem that when one man brings to the knowledge of another some truth upon which he has meditated, such an act pertains to the contemplative life.

But he who prays for another in no way acts upon him for whom he prays; his acts are directed towards God alone, the Intelligible Truth. But he who teaches another does act upon him by some external action. Hence there is no parallel between the two cases.

IV

Does the Active Life continue after this Life?

S. Gregory says: "The active life passes away with this present world; the contemplative life begins here so as to be perfected in our heavenly home."

As already said, the active life makes its end consist in external actions, and these, if they are directed towards the repose of contemplation, already belong to the contemplative life. But in the future life of the blessed all occupation with external things will cease; or if there are any external acts they will be directed towards that end which is contemplation. Hence S. Augustine says, at the close of his *Of the City of God*: "There we shall be at rest from toil, we shall gaze, we shall love, we shall praise." And he had just previously said: "There will God be seen unendingly, be loved without wearying, be praised without fatigue; this duty, this disposition of soul, this act, will be the lot of all."

Some, however, maintain that the active life will be continued after this life, thus:

1. To the active life belong the acts of the moral virtues. But the moral virtues remain after death, as S. Augustine says.

But the acts of the moral virtues which are concerned with the means to the end will not remain after death, but only those which have to do with the end itself. Yet it is precisely these latter which go to form the repose of contemplation to which S. Augustine alludes in the above-quoted passage where he speaks of being "at rest from toil"; and this "rest" is not to be understood of freedom from merely external disturbances, but also from the internal conflict of the passions.

2. Again, to teach others pertains to the active life. But in the next life—where we shall be as the Angels—there can be teaching; for we see it in the case of the Angels of whom one illumines, clarifies, and perfects another, all of which refer to their reception of knowledge, as is clear from Denis the Areopagite. Hence it seems that the active life is to be continued after this life.

But the contemplative life especially consists in the contemplation of God; and as regards this no Angel teaches another, for it is said of the Angels of *the little ones*—Angels who are of an inferior choir—that *they always see the face of the Father*. And similarly in the future life: there no man will teach another about God, for we shall all *see Him as He is*. And this agrees with the words of Jeremias: *And they shall teach no more every man his neighbour ... saying: Know the Lord; for all shall know Me from the least of them even to the greatest.*

97

But when it is question of dispensing the mysteries of God, then one Angel can teach another by clarifying, illumining, and perfecting. And in this sense the Angels do in some sort share in the active life as long as this world lasts, for they are occupied with ministering to the inferior creation. This is what was signified by Jacob's vision of the Angels ascending the ladder—whereby was meant the contemplative life—and descending the ladder—whereby was meant the active life. At the same time, as S. Gregory says: "Not that they so went out from the Divine Vision as to be deprived of the joys of contemplation." And thus in their case the active life is not distinguished from the contemplative as it is in us who find the works of the active life an impediment to the contemplative life. Moreover, we are not promised a likeness to the Angels in their work of administering to the inferior creation, for this does not belong to us according to our nature, as is the case with the Angels, but according to our vision of God.

3. Lastly, the more durable a thing is the more capable it seems of lasting after this life. But the active life is more durable than the contemplative, for S. Gregory says: "We can remain steadfast in the active life, but in nowise can we maintain the mind's fixed gaze in the contemplative life." Consequently the active life is much more capable of continuing after death than is the contemplative life.

But in our present state the durability of the active life as compared with the contemplative life does not arise from any feature of either of these kinds of life considered in themselves, but from a defect on our part; for we are dragged down from the heights of contemplation by the body's burden. And thus S. Gregory goes on to say that, "thrust back by its very weakness from those vast heights, the soul relapses into itself."

"O bless our God, ye Gentiles: and make the voice of His praise to be heard. Who hath set my soul to live: and hath not suffered my feet to be moved. For Thou, O God, hast proved us; Thou hast tried us by fire, as silver is tried. Thou hast brought us into a net, Thou hast laid afflictions on our back; Thou hast set men over our heads. We have passed through fire and water, and Thou hast brought us out into a refreshment."

QUESTION CLXXXII

OF THE COMPARISON BETWEEN THE ACTIVE AND THE CONTEMPLATIVE LIFE

I

Is the Active Life preferable to the Contemplative?

The Lord said: *Mary hath chosen the best part, which shall not be taken away from her.* And by Mary is signified the contemplative life, which is consequently to be preferred to the active.

There is no reason why one thing should not be in itself more excellent than another while yet this latter is, for certain reasons, preferable to it. Absolutely speaking, then, the contemplative life is better than the active. And the Philosopher alleges eight proofs of this. Firstly, that the contemplative life pertains to that which is best in a man, namely his intellect and its proper objects, *i.e.* intelligible truths, whereas the active life is concerned with external things. Hence Rachel, who typifies the contemplative life, is interpreted as meaning "the Beginning seen"; while Lia, who was blear-eyed, typifies, according to S. Gregory, the active life.

Secondly, because the contemplative life can be more continuous, even though we cannot maintain our contemplation at its highest pitch; thus Mary, who is typical of the contemplative life, is depicted as sitting ever at the Lord's feet.

Thirdly, because the delights of the contemplative life surpass those of the active life; whence S. Augustine says: "Martha was troubled, but Mary feasted."

Fourthly, because in the contemplative life a man is more independent, since for this kind of life he needs less; whence we read: *Martha, Martha, thou art careful, and art troubled about many things.*

Fifthly, because the contemplative life is loved rather for its own sake, whereas the active life is directed towards an end other than itself; whence it is said in Ps. xxvi. 4: *One thing I have asked of the Lord, this will I seek after, that I may dwell in the house of the Lord all the days of my life.*

Sixthly, because the contemplative life consists in a certain stillness and repose, as is said in Ps. xlv. II: *Be still, and see that I am God.*

Seventhly, because the contemplative life is occupied with Divine things whereas the active life is occupied with human things; whence S. Augustine says: "In the beginning was the Word: see What Mary heard! The Word was made Flesh; see to What Martha ministered!"

Eighthly, because the contemplative life pertains to that which is more peculiar to man—namely, his intellect—whereas in the works of the active life our inferior powers—those, namely, which we share with the brute creation—have a part; whence, in Ps. xxxv. 7, after

99

saying: *Beasts and men Thou wilt preserve, O Lord,* the Psalmist adds what belongs to men alone: *In Thy light we shall see light.*

And the Lord Himself gives a ninth reason when He says: *Mary hath chosen the best part which shall not be taken away from her,* words which S. Augustine thus expounds: "Not that thou, Martha, hast chosen badly, but that Mary hath chosen better; and see in what sense she hath chosen better: because it *shall not be taken away from her,* for from thee shall one day be taken away the burden of necessity; but eternal is the sweetness of truth."

But in a certain sense, and in certain cases, the active life is to be chosen in preference to the contemplative, and this by reason of the needs of this present life; as also the Philosopher says: "To practise philosophy is better than to become rich; but to become rich is better for one who suffers need."

Some, however, think that the active life is preferable to the contemplative, thus:

1. "The lot which falls to the better people seems to be the more honourable and better," as the Philosopher says. But the active life is the lot of those who are in the higher position—of prelates, for instance, who are placed in honourable and powerful positions; thus S. Augustine says: "In the life of action we must not love the honour which belongs to this life, nor its power." Whence it would seem that the active life is preferable to the contemplative.

But it is not the active life only which belongs to prelates, they must needs excel in the contemplative life; whence S. Gregory says in his *Pastoral Rule:* "Let the superior be foremost in action, but before all let him be uplifted in contemplation."

2. Again, in all acts and habits the control belongs to the more important: the soldier, for instance—as being higher placed—directs the saddle-maker. But it is the active life which directs and controls the contemplative, as is clear from the words addressed to Moses: *Go down and charge the people, lest they should have a mind to pass the limits to see the Lord.* The active life is therefore more important than the contemplative.

But the contemplative life consists in a certain liberty of spirit; for S. Gregory says: "The contemplative life means passing over to a certain liberty of spirit since in it a man thinks not of temporal but of eternal things." Similarly Boëthius says: "The human soul must needs be free when occupied with the thought of the Divine Mind; not so when distracted with the things of the body." From all this it is clear that the active life does not directly guide the contemplative, but by preparing the way for it it does direct certain works pertaining to the contemplative life, and in this sense the active life is rather the servant than the master of the contemplative. And this S. Gregory expresses when he says: "The active life is termed a service, the contemplative life freedom."

3. Lastly, no one should be withdrawn from what is greater in order to apply himself to what is less; thus the Apostle says: *Be zealous for the better gifts.* But some are withdrawn from the

contemplative state of life and are made to busy themselves with the affairs of the active life; this is the case, for instance, with those who are placed in positions of authority. Whence it seems that the active life is of more importance than the contemplative.

But though a man may happen to be called away from contemplation to the works of the active life owing to the needs of the present life, yet he is not thereby compelled completely to relinquish his contemplation. Hence S. Augustine says: "The love of truth asks for a holy leisure; the demands of charity undertake honest toil—that, namely, of the active life. And if no one imposes this latter burden on us, then we must devote ourselves to the study and contemplation of the truth; if, however, such a burden is imposed upon us, then must we undertake it because of the demands of charity. Yet not even then are we altogether to resign the joys flowing from the contemplation of truth, lest the sweetness of such contemplation be withdrawn from us and the burden we have assumed crush us."

Whence it appears that when a man is called from the contemplative to the active life it is not so much that something is withdrawn from him, but that an additional burden is imposed upon him.

"As we have heard, so have we seen, in the city of the Lord of Hosts, in the city of our God: God hath founded it for ever. We have received Thy mercy, O God, in the midst of Thy temple. For this is God, our God unto eternity, and for ever and ever: He shall rule us for evermore."

Cajetan: Those whose duty it is to instruct others in spiritual progress should note that they are bound to take great pains to exercise them in the active life before they urge them to ascend the heights of contemplation. For they must learn to subdue their passions by acquiring habits of meekness, patience, generosity, humility, and tranquillity of soul, before they ascend to the contemplative life. Through lack of this, many, not so much walking in the way of God as leaping along it, find themselves—after they have spent the greater portion of their life in contemplation—devoid of virtue, impatient, irascible, and proud, if one but so much as touch them on this point! Such people have neither the active nor the contemplative life, nor even a mixture of the two; they have built upon sand! And would that such cases were rare! (*on* 2. 182. 1 2.).

S. Augustine: Terrified by my sins and my weight of misery I was disturbed within my soul and meditated flight into solitude. But Thou didst forbid it and didst strengthen me and say: *Christ died for all, that they also who live may not now live to themselves, but unto Him Who died for them and rose again.* Behold, O Lord, I cast my care upon Thee so that I may live, and I will meditate on the wondrous things of Thy law. Thou knowest my lack of skill and my weakness; teach me and heal me! He—Thine Only-Begotten Son—in Whom lie hid all the treasures of wisdom and knowledge, He redeemed me with His blood. *Let not the proud calumniate me!* When I think of my Ransom then I eat and I drink, and I pray, and in my poverty I yearn to be filled with Him, to be among those who *eat and are filled* and they *praise the Lord who seek Him* (*Conf.*, X., xliii. 70).

S. Augustine: He hath hid me in His tabernacle in the day of evils.

Wherefore without any arrogance have I sought for That One Thing, neither doth my soul reproach me, saying: Why do you seek after It? From whom do you seek It? Do you, a sinner, wickedly dare to ask something of God? Do you, weak man, of unclean heart, dare to hope that you will one day attain to the contemplation of God? I dare! Not indeed of myself, but because of His pleasure in me; not out of presumptuous trust in myself, but from confidence in His promise. For will He Who gave such a pledge to the pilgrim desert him when he comes to Him? *For He hath hid me in His tabernacle in the day of evils* (*Enarr. in Ps.* xxvi.).

II

Is the Active Life more Meritorious than the Contemplative?

S. Gregory says: "Great are the merits of the active life, but they are surpassed by those of the contemplative life."

The source of merit is charity. Charity, however, consists in the love of God and of our neighbour; and to love God is, in itself, more meritorious than to love our neighbour. Consequently that which more directly pertains to the love of God is more meritorious in its nature than something that directly pertains to the love of our neighbour for God's sake. The contemplative life, however, directly and immediately pertains to the love of God, as S. Augustine says: "The love of truth asks for a holy leisure; that is the contemplative life," and this truth is the Divine Truth on Which the contemplative life is centred. The active life, on the other hand, is more immediately concerned with the love of our neighbour, it is *busy about much serving*. Hence of its very nature the contemplative life is more meritorious than the active, as is well expressed by S. Gregory when he says: "The contemplative life is more meritorious than the active, for the latter toils in the wear and tear of present work by which it must needs help its neighbour; whereas the former, by a certain inward savour, already has a foretaste of the repose to come"—that is, in the contemplation of God.

It may, however, chance that one man derives greater merit from the works of the active life than another does from his contemplative life; as, for example, when, from the superabundance of the Divine love, in order to fulfil God's will, and for His greater glory, a man is content to be separated for a space from the sweetness of Divine contemplation, as the Apostle says: *I wished myself to be an anathema from Christ for my brethren.* On these words S. Chrysostom comments thus: "The love of Christ had so completely taken possession of his heart that he could even despise that which he desired beyond all things—namely, to be with Christ—and that because it was pleasing to Christ."

Yet some maintain that the active life is more meritorious than the contemplative, thus:

I. A thing is said to be meritorious because of the reward. But reward is due to work, as S. Paul says: *And every man shall receive his own reward according to his own labour.* Labour, however, belongs to the active life, repose to the contemplative, as S. Gregory says: "Everyone who is converted to God must needs first labour in toil; he must take Lia—that is, that so he may arrive at 'the vision of the Beginning'—that is, the embraces of Rachel." Whence it seems as though the active life was more meritorious than the contemplative.

But while external toil makes for an increase of accidental reward, the increase of merit as regards essential reward consists mainly in charity, one proof of which is external toil undertaken for Christ's sake; but a much greater proof of this is given when a man puts aside all that pertains to this life and delights in giving himself up solely to Divine contemplation.

2. Again, contemplative life is in some sort the commencement of future bliss; and consequently the words of S. John: *So will I have him to remain till I come*, S. Augustine comments as follows: "This might be more fully expressed thus: May perfect actions, modelled on the example of My Passion, follow Me; but may contemplation begun here on earth remain till I come, to be perfected when I come"; and similarly S. Gregory says: "The contemplative life begins here below to be perfected in our heavenly home." But in that future life we shall not merit, but shall receive the reward of our merits. Consequently the contemplative life seems to have less of the ratio of merit than has the active life; but it has more of the ratio of reward.

But in the state of future bliss a man has arrived at his perfection and consequently there is no room left for merit; but if there were room left his merits would be more efficacious owing to the pre-eminence of his charity. The contemplation of this present life, however, has some accompanying imperfection, and consequently there is room for improvement; hence such contemplation does not destroy the idea of meriting but makes increase of merit in proportion as Divine charity is more and more exercised.

3. Lastly, S. Gregory says: "No sacrifice is more acceptable to God than zeal for souls." But zeal for souls means that a man gives himself up to the works of the active life. Whence it seems that the contemplative life is not more meritorious than the active.

But a sacrifice is spiritually offered to God when anything is presented to Him; and of all man's good things God specially accepts that of the human soul when offered to Him in sacrifice. But a man ought to offer to God first of all his own soul, according to the words of Ecclesiasticus: *Have pity on thine own soul, pleasing God;* secondly, the souls of others, according to the words: *And he that heareth let him say: Come.* But the more closely a man knits his own soul, or his neighbour's soul, to God, the more acceptable to God is his sacrifice; consequently it is more pleasing to God that a man should give his soul, and the souls of others, to contemplation than to action. When, then, S. Gregory says: "No sacrifice is more acceptable to God than zeal for souls," he does not mean that the merit of the active life is greater than that of the contemplative, but that it is more meritorious that a man should offer to God his own soul and the soul of others than that he should offer any other external gift whatsoever.

"But thou, our God, art gracious and true, patient, and ordering all things in mercy. For if we sin, we are Thine, knowing Thy greatness: and if we sin not, we know that we are counted with Thee. For to know Thee is perfect justice: and to know Thy justice, and Thy power, is the root of immortality."

III

Is the Active Life a Hindrance to the Contemplative Life?

S. Gregory says: "They who would hold the citadel of contemplation must first needs exercise themselves on the battle-field of toil."

We may consider the active life from two points of view. For we may first of all consider the actual occupation with, and practice of, external works; and from this point of view it is clear that the active life is a hindrance to the contemplative, for it is impossible for a man to be simultaneously occupied with external works, and yet at leisure for Divine contemplation.

But we may also consider the active life from the standpoint of the harmony and order which it introduces into the interior passions of the soul; and from this point of view the active life is an assistance to contemplation since this latter is hindered by the disturbance arising from the passions. Thus S. Gregory says: "They who would hold the citadel of contemplation must first needs exercise themselves on the battle-field of toil; they must learn, forsooth, whether they still do harm to their neighbours, whether they bear with equanimity the harm their neighbours may do them; whether, when temporal good things are set before them, their minds are overwhelmed with joy; whether when such things are withdrawn they are over much grieved. And lastly, they must ask themselves whether, when they withdraw within upon themselves and search into the things of the spirit, they do not carry with them the shadows of things corporeal, or whether, if perchance they have touched upon them, they discreetly repel them."

Thus, then, the exercises of the active life are conducive to contemplation, for they still those interior passions whence arise those imaginations which serve as a hindrance to contemplation.

Some, however, maintain that the active life is a hindrance to the contemplative, thus:

1. A certain stillness of mind is needful for contemplation, as the Psalmist says: *Be still and see that I am God.* But the active life implies anxiety: *Martha, Martha, thou art careful, and art troubled about many things.*

2. Again, a certain clearness of vision is called for in the contemplative life. But the active life hinders this clearness of vision, for S. Gregory says: "Lia was blear-eyed and fruitful, for the active life, since occupied with toil, sees less clearly."

3. And lastly, things that are contrary hinder one another. But the active and the contemplative life are contrary to one another; for the active life is occupied with many things, whereas the contemplative life dwells upon one object of contemplation; they are, then, in opposite camps.

But all these arguments insist upon the occupation with external affairs which is but one feature in the active life, not upon its other feature—namely, its power to repress the passions.

Cajetan: But the five foolish virgins, having taken their lamps, did not take oil with them. But the wise took oil in their vessels with the lamps.

By this oil is signified testimony to a man's goodness or love of God. For there is this difference between people who perform good works, that the only testimony which some men have to their goodness is without—namely, in the works themselves; within, however, they do not feel that they love God with their whole heart, that they repent of their sins because they are hateful to God, or that they love their neighbour for God's sake. But there are others who so perform good works that both their works that shine before men bear witness without to the good soul within, and also within their own conscience the Holy Spirit Himself testifies to their spirit that they are the sons of God; for such men feel that they love God with their whole heart, that they repent of their sins for God's sake, and that they love their neighbour and themselves for God's sake: in brief, they feel that God is the sole reason why they love, why they hope, fear, rejoice, or are sad: in a word, why they work both within and without: this is to have oil in one's own vessels (*On S. Matt.* xxv. 3, 4).

S. Augustine: See the life that Mary chose! Yet was she but a type of that life, she as yet possessed it not. For there are two kinds of life: one means delight; the other means a burden. And the burdensome one is toilsome, while the delightsome one is pleasurable. But enter thou within; seek not that delight without, lest ye swell with it and find yourself unable to enter by the narrow gate! See how Mary saw the Lord in the Flesh and heard the Lord by the voice of the Flesh—as ye have heard when the Epistle to the Hebrews has been read—as it were through a veil. (*A new and living way which He hath dedicated to us through the veil, that is to say, His Flesh.*) But when we shall see Him face to Face there will be no "veil." Mary, then, sat—that is, she rested from toil—and she listened and she praised; but Martha was anxious about much serving. And the Lord said to her: *Martha, Martha, thou art careful and art troubled about many things; but one thing is necessary* (*Sermon,* CCLVI., v. 6).

"Bless the Lord, O my soul: and let all that is within me bless His holy Name. Bless the Lord, O my soul, and never forget all He hath done for thee. Who forgiveth all thy iniquities: Who healeth all thy diseases. Who redeemeth thy life from destruction: Who crowneth thee with mercy and compassion. Who satisfieth thy desire with good things: thy youth shall be renewed like the eagle's. The Lord doth mercies, and judgment for all that suffer wrong. He hath made His ways known to Moses: His wills to the children of Israel. The Lord is compassionate and merciful: long suffering and plenteous in mercy. He will not always be angry: nor will He threaten for ever. He hath not dealt with us according to our sins: nor rewarded us according to our iniquities. For according to the height of the Heaven above the earth: He hath strengthened His mercy towards them that fear Him. As far as the east is from the west, so far hath He removed our iniquities from us. As a father hath compassion on his children, so hath the Lord compassion on them that fear Him: for He knoweth our frame. He remembereth that we are dust: man's days are as grass, as the flower of the field so shall he flourish."

IV

Does the Active Life precede the Contemplative?

S. Gregory says: "The active life precedes the contemplative in the order of time, for from good works a man passes to contemplation."

One thing may precede another in two ways: firstly by its very nature; and in this sense the contemplative life precedes the active in that it is occupied with chiefer and better things, and hence it both moves and directs the active life. For, as S. Augustine says, the higher reason, which is destined for contemplation, is compared to the lower reason, which is destined for action, as man is compared to woman—she is to be governed by him.

But secondly, one thing may be prior to another as far as we are concerned, it may, that is, precede it in the way of generation. And in this sense the active life precedes the contemplative, for it conduces to it, as we have already said. In the order of generation disposition to a nature precedes that nature, though that nature is, simply speaking and considered in itself, prior to the disposition to it.

But some maintain that the active life does not precede the contemplative, thus:

1. The contemplative life is directly concerned with the love of God, the active life with the love of our neighbour. But love of God precedes love of our neighbour, for we have to love our neighbour for God's sake.

But the contemplative life is not concerned with merely any kind of love of God, but with the perfect love of Him; the active life, on the contrary, is necessary for any kind of love of our neighbour, for S. Gregory says: "Without the contemplative life men can gain admittance to their heavenly home if they have not neglected the good works they could have done; but they cannot enter without the active life, if they neglect the good works they could do." Whence it appears that the active life precedes the contemplative in the sense that that which is common to everybody precedes in the order of generation that which is peculiar to the perfect.

2. Again, S. Gregory says: "You must know that just as the right procedure is for a man to pass from the active to the contemplative life; so, too, it is often profitable to the soul to return to the active life." Consequently the active life is not absolutely speaking prior to the contemplative.

But while we proceed from the active life to the contemplative by way of generation, we return from the contemplative to the active by way of direction, in order, that is, that our active life may be directed by the contemplative; just in the same way as habits are generated by acts and then, as is said in the *Ethics*, when the habit is formed we act still more perfectly.

3. Lastly, things which accord with different characters do not seem to be necessarily related. But the active and contemplative life are suited to different characters; thus S. Gregory says: "It often happens that men who could have given themselves to peaceful contemplation of God have been burdened with external occupations and so have made shipwreck; while, on the contrary, men who could have lived well had they been occupied with human concerns, have been slain by the sword of their life of repose." Consequently the active life does not seem to precede the contemplative.

But those who are subject to the influx of their passions because of their natural eagerness in action, are for that very reason more suited for the active life, and this because of the restlessness of their temperament. Hence S. Gregory says: "Some are so restless that if they desist from work they suffer grievously, for the more free they are to think the worse interior tumults they have to endure." Some, on the contrary, have a natural purity of soul and a reposefulness which renders them fit for the contemplative life; if such men were to be applied wholly to the active life they would incur great loss. Hence S. Gregory says: "Some men are of so slothful a disposition that if they undertake any work they succumb at the very outset." But he adds: "Yet often love stirs up even slothful souls to work, and fear exercises a restraining influence on souls which suffer a disturbing influence in their contemplation." Hence even those who are more suited for the active life, may, by the exercise of it, be prepared for the contemplative; and, on the contrary, those who are more suited for the contemplative life may profitably undertake the labours proper to the active life, that so they may be rendered still more fit for contemplation.

"I have cried to Thee, for Thou, O God, hast heard me: O incline Thy ear unto me, and hear my words. Show forth Thy wonderful mercies; Thou Who savest them that trust in Thee. From them that resist Thy right hand keep me, as the apple of Thy eye. Protect me under the shadow of Thy wings."

QUESTION CLXXXVI

ON THE RELIGIOUS STATE

Are Contemplative Orders superior to Active Orders?

The Lord declared that Mary's was *the best part*, and she is the type of the contemplative life.

Religious Orders differ from one another primarily according to the ends they have in view, but secondarily according to the works they practise. And since one thing cannot be said to be superior to another save by reason of the differences between them, it will follow that the superiority of one Religious Order to another must depend primarily upon their respective ends, secondarily upon the works they practise.

And these two grounds of comparison are not of equal value; for the comparison between them from the point of view of their respective ends is an absolute one, since an end is sought for its own sake; whereas the comparison arising from their respective works is a relative one, since works are not done for their own sake but for the sake of the end to be gained.

Consequently one Religious Order is superior to another if its end is absolutely a superior one, either as being in itself a greater good, or as being of wider scope. On the supposition, however, that the ends of any two Orders are the same, then the superiority of one to the other can be gauged, not by the quantity of works they undertake, but by the proportion these bear to the end in view. Thus it is that we find introduced into the *Conferences of the Fathers* the opinion of S. Antony, who preferred that discretion by which a man moderates all things to fasts and watchings and similar observances.

The works, then, of the active life are twofold. There is one which springs from the fulness of contemplation: teaching, for example, and preaching. Whence S. Gregory says: "It is said of perfect men that on their return from contemplation: *They shall pour forth the memory of Thy sweetness.*" And this is preferable to simple contemplation. For just as it is a greater thing to shed light than to be full of light, so is it a greater thing to spread abroad the fruits of our contemplation than merely to contemplate. And the second work of the active life is that which wholly consists in external occupation, such as giving alms, receiving guests, etc. And such works are inferior to the works of contemplation, except it be in some case of necessity.

Consequently, then, those Religious Orders are in the highest rank which are devoted to teaching and preaching. And these, too, approach most nearly to the perfection of the Episcopate; just as in other things, too, the ends of those in the first place are, as S. Denis says, close knit to the principles of those in the second place. The second rank is occupied by those Orders which are devoted to contemplation. And the third with those devoted to external works.

And in each of these grades there is a certain superiority according as one Order aims at acts of a higher order than does another, though of the same class. Thus in the works of the active life it is a greater thing to redeem captives than to receive guests; in the contemplative life, too, it is a greater thing to pray than to study. There may also be a certain superiority in this that one is occupied with more of such works than another; or again, that the rules of one are better adapted to the attainment of their end than are those of another.

Some, however, maintain that the contemplative Orders are not superior to the active Orders, thus:

1. In the Canon Law it is said: "Since the greater good is to be preferred to the less, so, too, the common gain is to be preferred to private gain; and in this sense teaching is rightly preferred to silence, anxious care for others to contemplation, and toil to repose." But that Religious Order is the better which is directed to the attainment of the greater good. Hence it seems that Orders which are devoted to an active life are superior to those which aim solely at contemplation.

But this Decretal speaks of the active life as concerned with the salvation of souls.

2. All Religious Orders aim at the perfection of charity. But on those words in the Epistle to the Hebrews, *Ye have not yet resisted unto blood*, the Gloss has: "There is no more perfect charity in this life than that to which the holy Martyrs attained, for they strove against sin even *unto blood*." But to strive *unto blood* belongs to the Military Religious Orders, and they lead an active life. It would seem, then, that these latter are the highest form of Religious Order. But these Military Orders are more concerned with shedding the blood of their enemies than with shedding their own, which is the feature of the Martyrs. At the same time, there is nothing to preclude these Religious from at times winning the crown of martyrdom and thus attaining to a greater height than other Religious; just as in some cases active works are to be preferred to contemplation.

3. Lastly, the stricter an Order the more perfect it seems to be. But there is nothing to preclude active Orders from being stricter in their observance than some contemplative Orders.

But strictness of observance is not that which is especially commendable in Religious life, as S. Antony has already told us, and as is also said in Isaias: *Is this such a fast as I have chosen, for a man to afflict his soul for a day?* Strictness of observance is, however, made use of in Religious Orders for the subjection of the flesh; but if such strictness is carried out without discretion there is danger lest it should come to naught, as S. Antony says. Hence one Religious Order is not superior to another because its observances are stricter, but because its observances are directed to the end of that Order with greater discretion. Thus, for example, abstinence from food and drink, which means hunger and thirst, are more efficacious means for preserving chastity than wearing less clothing, which means cold and nakedness; more efficacious, too, than bodily labour.

39922208R00066

Made in the USA
Middletown, DE
21 March 2019